I0533973

WESTWARD JOURNEY

Anastasia S. Tarkington

WESTWARD JOURNEY

To my Lord and Savior,
Jesus Christ, from whom all blessings flow
(Proverbs 3:9)

WESTWARD JOURNEY

Colleen was up and out the door in no time, the next morning. A pair of pants and a big shirt lay out for her, though there was no sign of her ma who was, on most occasions the first one up in the morning. Colleen dressed hurriedly in the shirt and as strange as they felt, the pants. She pinned up her hair and added one of her pa's hats with a wide brim to the clothes she would now have to wear every day. She ate a quick breakfast, and, relying on the hope that her ma would remind Joey that he would have to do all the chores today, saddled Daisy and rode off before anyone else awoke. She reached Morristown in time to see the sunrise between the two green hills south of the town, and was ready to face the day . . . like a man, so to speak.

Right as she was making her way to the General Store, she jumped down from Daisy's back and scooped up a handful of dirt to smear across her face and chin to give her a scruffy look. Then she walked, head up, shoulders back, guiding Daisy to the General Store and tying her up where she'd have plenty of shade the whole day.

Colleen had never before been in town so early and was amazed by how many people were out and about during a rancher's chore time. And just when she'd thought the nervousness had gone away, this reminded Colleen that the more people she saw, the more people she would have to try to avoid so no one would recognize her.

WESTWARD JOURNEY

WESTWARD JOURNEY

WESTWARD JOURNEY

ONE

The summer sun shined down on the little prairie village of Morristown. Farmers traded their goods and visited the General Store for groceries and small trinkets. Horse hooves sounded hard on the packed dirt road before the General Store. Wagon wheels squeaked, a rooster crowed somewhere in one of the shop owner's' backyards. Farmer's wives bustled around chatting and keeping up with their mischievous and numerous children who ran around the small town annoying some, but mostly just making everyone laugh, making the older folks wish they had the same amount of energy.

The town wasn't made up of just nearby farm owners and store clerks though, actually most of the people who came into town were farmers or ranchers who lived several miles out. And of course those farmers and ranchers had wives and even bigger families than the ones that lived in town. Because, of course, the more the children there were, the more people there were to help with the the chores on the farm.

Some of those families were the Lathans, the Hollisters, the McCaslins, and the Northams. The rumor in town was that Ellie Hollister and Colleen Northam were the prettiest girls around. And of course as they got older their parents knew to be aware of the oncoming assembly of young men that were sure to be calling soon. Ellie Hollister was fine with the idea, and as a matter of fact was already rather taken with young Arnie McCaslin. Colleen Northam, on the other hand, wasn't so sure about the idea of callers — which would eventually lead to marriage — but in all the books she read, it was her favorite part. So perhaps callers wouldn't be too bad after all.

Colleen's parents, Jethro and Anne Northam were godly, hardworking people and good neighbors too. And to be truthful, they weren't too excited about the idea that their Colleen could be marrying and leaving home in a year or less. But they understood that for everything there is a season and that the final decision would rest with Colleen on the matter. "It's her doing the marryin'," Jethro said to Anne during one of their late night discussions about it. "How about we let her and the good Lord decide who and when it will be." Anne had nodded her agreement and the matter was considered settled. And so far, nothing had happened. It wasn't that no one showed interest, but that no one made any moves. So Colleen kept growing prettier and gaining more knowledge on how to go about someday making her own home.

Mr. Northam owned a cattle ranch several miles from Morristown and the year for the cattle had been a good one although lately it had been dry, due to little rain that spring. The herd looked promising though and Colleen could tell that her pa was excited to take them to market just as soon as it was time. Several times a day she helped him haul water for the cattle. She helped her mother mend clothing and clean their small house. She had just started preparing more of the family's meals throughout the week because everyone liked her dish of mashed potatoes, chicken, and biscuits and gravy so much. "Besides," her mother had told her, "one day you'll be making all your family's meals. It's time you start practicing." Of course anytime her mother said this, it would just bring on a smile from Colleen and she would say, "Oh, Ma. Cooking for two would be a dream compared to cooking for seven." To which her mother would playfully respond; "But not as many people to tell you how good the meal was." Then they would share a good laugh together.

One of Colleen's favorite parts of each day was when she would ride out with her father to check the cattle. She was a very experienced rider for her age and reading and riding were her two favorite things to do. And although her pa was the happiest man around, and super proud of his daughter's riding abilities, every year for the annual town fair Colleen tried to talk him into letting her ride in the horse race. And even though he wondered sometimes what would happen if he did, he always told her no because with every passing year, the cowboys who raced seemed to get rougher and rougher. Hardly even minding the rules of the race. Yet even knowing this, his sweet Colleen still wanted to race. And if it wasn't for her mother's strong opinion on the matter, Jethro might have given in by now.

Colleen rode with her pa, rounding up and checking all the cattle before the day was considered finished. Even with her bonnet on and her hair pulled up tightly, she could still feel little drops of sweat running down her back and dampening her blouse. The sun shined swelteringly above and gave everything a hazy look. Colleen looked towards the creek. *Even the trees looked hot*, Collen thought as she watched some of the smaller branches bend and sway in a sudden, hot breeze. She wished the breeze would blow in the beautiful signs and cooler weather of autumn already. However, she knew her pa would need the warmer weather to hang on for just a little while longer so that he could take the cattle to market. The cattle were in good condition this year, her pa had said that this may be one of their best years yet. In just a few weeks — after the annual fair — her pa would be leaving on his eight week long trip, along with some other cattle hands he would hire to help him drive the herd to market. If winter came too soon, he would have a rough journey back, so Colleen decided to be content with the weather just as it was.

"Alright, Colleen!" her pa called across from the other side of the herd, "Let's call it a night!"

Colleen nodded and turned her horse, Daisy towards the log cabin that was home. She already missed these evenings spent with her pa while he would be away. And she would continue to miss them until he and the cattle hands were back from their exhausting trip to the market. She wondered if her pa would get some of the same men to work for him this year as he did last year. He had been so thankful that all the men he had hired to help him drive the cattle to market were hardworking and loyal men. With cattle ranches, finding loyal men was one of the most difficult, yet important parts of the job.

Colleen rode along with her father back towards the house. As they rode, she turned in her saddle for one last look at the cattle. After seeing that all was well, she turned back around again. When they got back to the house, Colleen followed her pa into the barn to unsaddle the horses and rub them down before starting in on the evening chores. After Colleen had groomed and fed Daisy, she went to milk the cow and feed the pigs before washing up and going in the house to help her ma get supper ready. On her way in the house, her pa called after her like he always did, "Thank you for helping me, Colleen." She turned and smiled at her pa. "You're welcome." It wasn't much later that the potatoes were peeled, the sausage fried, the bread cut, and the table set; and then supper was on the kitchen table and the family was gathered around, saying a prayer over the food and beginning to eat.

Colleen took a bite of bread, her thoughts not really being on the meal before her. The boys — Joey, Aaron, and Riley — all looked at her wonderingly as they downed their food in big, satisfying bites. Even little Abigail Rose seemed to look at her questioningly as she chewed on her piece of bread. Finally, Colleen couldn't stand to wait any longer. She had to ask just one last time.

"Pa, don't you think I could enter in the race this year? I'm a good rider. I'm sure they'd let me," she said. She looked at her pa who looked at her ma and sighed.

"I just don't think you should, Colleen," he said and Colleen's heart sank. "The men who ride in that race aren't the type of men I would want you to be around. They're there for a prize, not to be gentlemen."

"But don't you always say that we shouldn't judge people just by their appearance?" She asked him.

Her pa sighed. "Yes, that's true, but we still have to be careful. A single person who doesn't abide by the laws can tip the scale for everyone else. Even if you play by the rules of the game, you can't play for everyone else, which means that you won't know what they'll do. Every year that race gets rougher, Colleen. I just don't want you get hurt. That's why I don't want you to race." Colleen looked down at her plate sadly.

"I'm not saying that you can't go and watch the race," her pa said. "Actually, I think I'll take the day off here and we'll all go. We'll make a day of it."

"Can we take a picnic lunch too?" Aaron asked excitedly.

"We can," pa answered. "What do you say?"

"Well," ma said smiling, "I have been saving some ingredients for cookies, for a special occasion like this. I think it's a good idea."

Colleen smiled and nodded in agreement, as Abigail Rose cooed from her high chair. Even though she wanted so badly to be a part of the race herself, Colleen knew she would have to settle for just watching again this year. And it wasn't so bad, the more she thought about it because at least she would be going with her family.

TWO

The day of the race dawned bright and early and Colleen couldn't have been happier to realize the temperature outside wasn't so high. Even though the sun still shone in the sky, it wasn't nearly as hot as it had been for the past few weeks. After the morning chores had been done and the breakfast dishes washed and dried, the team was hitched to the wagon. Her pa helped her ma up into the wagon and handed Abigail Rose to her before helping Colleen up and letting the three boys climb in. The ride to town didn't seem to take as long as it usually did in Colleen's opinion, but to the boys it was torturous to sit still that long, especially when there was something exciting coming at the end of the road. Finally, after a long time of listening to the wind, chirping birds, and the squeaky wagon wheels, Colleen nudged the boys and pointed up ahead of them. "Look!" she said.

The three boys practically jumped out of the wagon when they saw Morristown's shop buildings not far off. They started chattering excitedly and even Colleen, who was still a little down about not being able to race, couldn't help but smile at their enthusiasm. She watched as her ma and pa traded a knowing smile and then her pa said, "Alright, boys. Settle down until we get there."

The boys quieted down some, but not for long. Pa guided the team onto the main road and followed the crowd through town and out beyond the shop buildings where the horse race was to take place. As soon as they found a place to tie the horses and a good spot for their picnic later, they settled down to wait until the race started. They didn't have to wait long before the races. Colleen noticed that as pa said they were all rough looking men who lined up with their horses in anticipation of the race. Pa took the excited boys over closer to the fence that surrounded the race track and Colleen, holding little Abigail Rose, and her ma lingered a little ways back with some of the other women. They watched the racers prepare their horses and climb up into their saddles, awaiting the gunshot that would signal the long awaited start of the race.

Finally, when all the riders were ready, the shot sounded with an echo and the racers were off in a cloud of dust and with a cheer from the crowd. The race was magnificent. One beige mare pulled ahead of all the other horses in just the first couple of strides and although other horses tried to get ahead of her, the beige mare always seemed to have more energy and had a much faster pace than all the others. And at the end of the race, it was the mare and her rider who won the race winning the prize of the shiny silver cup.

Everyone clapped and cheered for the winner as the Mayor handed him the cup. Colleen was almost surprised to see that the winner was a young man on the tall side; he had light brown hair and a clean shaven face. However, the most surprising thing to Colleen was how much of a gentleman he seemed to be. He accepted the award graciously thanking the Mayor and then turning to pat his horse's neck. It seemed to Colleen that he was thanking his horse with that pat. No words were needed after the kind gesture.

She hadn't meant to stare at him but when the young man met her gaze through the crowd, she quickly looked away at something else before glancing back again to find him still looking at her. When their eyes met again, the young man looked away just as quickly as she had and Colleen watched him for a time to see if he would look at her again, but he never did.

The usual town fair activities resumed after that. Colleen's family settled down for their picnic lunch and after they had eaten their meal, her pa gave her some money and asked her if she would mind going and buying a small treat for the boys. Colleen distractedly said that she would, accepted the money, and went to stand in line to buy a bag of hard candies. While she waited for the people in line ahead of her to purchase what they wished, she suddenly caught herself looking vaguely around for the young cowboy who had won the race. The moment she realized what she was doing, she made herself stop it and focus on the people in front of her instead. She was just a few people back in the line when a man she guessed to be in his thirties approached her.

"Hello, ma'am," the man said. Colleen suddenly felt slightly uncomfortable about how this man had sought her out of the crowd.

"Hello," she said cautiously, glancing over his shoulder trying to see her family or her pa.

"What is your name?" the man asked.

Colleen looked at the man; black hair, beard, his rough manner, all of which reminded her for some reason of what her pa had said the night before, ". . . The type of men I wouldn't want you to be around," or something like that. She couldn't quite remember for sure as long as this man was demanding her attention. Still, she had no real reason to be wary of him, and her ma and pa had always taught her not to judge someone just by their appearance, so she answered "Colleen." However, she did decide not to give her last name just to be safe. Cattle rustlers were growing sneakier and sneakier nowadays and they would do just about anything to steal cattle while the rancher was caught off guard.

"And where would I go about to see you later?" the man asked stepping towards her.

"Me?" Colleen smelled whiskey or some other alcoholic drink on the man's breath. She took a step back as she said, "Sir, I think really you should be asking my pa that."

"Well, I won't know who your pa is if you don't give me your last name," the man said stepping towards her again.

"Sir, please," she said as she took another step away from him, realizing that with each step the man was getting her further away from the crowd. "If you want to see my pa, then I'll take you to him," she told him. "He's right over there." She pointed over the man's shoulder as she finally spotted her pa in relief.

The man ignored where she was pointing to and laid a heavy hand on her shoulder, saying, "I want to ask *you*." The man leaned towards her but Colleen had no time to think, step away, or even scream, because just at that moment, a hand was laid on the man's shoulder and someone pulled him away from Colleen and slammed him up against the store wall behind her in one quick movement.

Colleen almost cried from the relief that her pa had seen her and came to rescue her, when she saw that the man who had the other man pinned up against the wall wasn't her father. It was the cowboy who had won the race. He had the other man by the shoulders, pinning him against the wall, his face leaned in close so that the man couldn't really look anywhere else but this strange young man's face.

"The lady said *please*," the cowboy said through clenched teeth. The other man swallowed hard and nodded, sweat trickling down his face.

"Colleen!" she heard her pa's voice but couldn't see him through the crowd that had suddenly gathered to watch.

"Now get outta here," the cowboy said letting go of the man and stepping back a little. The man nodded again, more in defiance this time, and, adjusting his coat, went on his way with one last look in Colleen's direction. Colleen watched him go, then slowly turned to the cowboy at a loss of words. The cowboy turned to her as the people around them tore their eyes away from what had just gone down. The cowboy lifted a hand to his hat, gave Colleen a small nod and turned and walked away. Too late, Colleen squeaked out a *thank you* to his back, that he didn't hear. A moment later, her pa's reassuring hand squeezed her shoulder and Colleen turned to face him in relief.

"Pa!" she exclaimed.

"Are you alright? What happened?" he asked putting protective arms around her.

"I'm fine, Pa," Colleen said trying to sort out what had just happened herself.

"Are you hurt?" her pa asked her again. "I saw a commotion over here but I couldn't get to you because the crowd was so thick. I think I elbowed some people to get them out of the way. Are you sure you're okay?"

"I'm fine, Pa. Really, I am," Colleen reassured him. She looked in her father's concerned face and forcingly smiled. She was a little shaken but was otherwise okay. However, she was confused as to why the cowboy would've helped her. Of course most gentlemen would and were expected to in that type of situation, but cowboys — especially racers, according to her father — didn't line up with the usual. Colleen smoothed out her dress and ran a hand over her hair to make sure it was still in place.

"The cowboy helped me," she told her pa quietly.

"Just as long as you're okay," her pa said hugging her tightly. "We'll have to find that cowboy and thank him. Do you know who he was?"

Colleen shook her head. "No, he didn't say anything." After a minute, she added, "He was the man who won the race."

Her pa looked at her closely, then put his arm around her shoulders and guided her away from the crowd. "Then I guess," he stopped and cleared his throat like he always did when he was nervous about something, "I guess I'll have to find him and thank him for keeping my baby girl safe." He squeezed her shoulder.

Colleen saw her family's picnic blanket just a few yards away and it reminded her of something she had forgotten in all the commotion. "Pa," she said turning to him, "I forgot. I never got to buy the candy."

Her pa smiled. "It's alright. I'll take care of it. You just stay here with your ma and the boys and little Abigail." Colleen nodded. She gave the money back to her pa and he turned to go but she said, "Pa," and he turned back to look at her.

"Yes?" he asked.

"Can we not tell ma?" she asked. "I'm afraid she won't let me out of the house again if she finds out."

Colleen's pa laughed and said, "You leave it to God and me. We'll find a way of explaining it to her."

Colleen nodded and turned back to her family's picnic blanket. When she got back to her family, the first thing her ma said was, "What happened? Your pa said something was up with the crowd and then jumped up and ran over to the stands like something was wrong." Colleen looked at her ma.

Slowly she said, "It's okay, Ma. Pa said that he was going to buy the—" Colleen almost said *candy* but caught herself just in time to say, "the surprise". Her ma looked at her pointedly and opened her mouth to say something but was interrupted by her approaching husband.

For the rest of the day, Colleen's ma held back from asking any more questions about what had happened. But that evening after Colleen and her siblings had already gone to bed, she heard her ma and pa talking in hushed voices, although she couldn't hear what it was that they were talking about. However, after that night, her mother never mentioned it to Colleen again, and

Colleen couldn't help but be grateful for it. Still, she sometimes thought of the young man who had come to her rescue when her father couldn't. And she prayed for the cowboy, thanking God that he had been there and asked God to reward him in some small way for it since she couldn't thank him properly.

THREE

Within three weeks of the race, it was obvious that summer would stay around for quite a while. Colleen's pa made plans to take the cattle to market the following week and was in the process of hiring some men to help him. He and Colleen were working harder than ever to watch the cattle and get them ready for the trip. Colleen was spending more time outside with her pa than she was inside with her ma. But that was perfectly fine with Colleen. The hot weather made it almost miserable to be outside for too long still, but the birds sung in the trees around their log cabin and the cattle lowed making a soothing sound in the background. Day and night, there was the sound of the wind whipping around their little farm on the prairie. Even with the heat and the mosquitoes, Colleen enjoyed being outside and spending the time with her pa and the animals.

One day though, less than a week before her pa was supposed to leave to take the cattle to market, the weather ended up being the last thing on Colleen's mind.

She had been helping her ma all day readying the garden for planting, and her pa had ridden out to check on the cattle alone. When the sun had made its way well toward the west, Colleen's ma brushed the dirt from her hands and dress and went in to start supper. After finishing up one last row, Colleen followed suit. On her way towards the house, she looked out towards the fields to see if her pa was coming, but there was no sign of him yet. Shaking the dirt out of her skirts, she walked into the house.

"Did you see your father?" her ma asked from where she stood at the stove.

"Not yet," Colleen answered as she poured some water to wash her hands with.

"Well, I think I'll send Joey out to call him. He hardly ever stays out so late," her ma said, "It must have been because he didn't have his helper today."

Colleen traded a smile with her ma as she went to call Joey to tell him to ride out and call his pa for supper. Colleen helped her ma with the food and was setting the table when she heard horse's hooves outside.

"That'll be them," her ma said. "Go out and tell them to hurry with the chores so we can eat." Colleen nodded and headed for the door. She was just reaching for the door handle when it burst open and there was Joey. His face was flushed and his hair was a mess from the wind during his ride, but it was the concerned look he was wearing and the wild look in his eyes that was so bewildering to Colleen.

"Joey," she said, about to tell him that he shouldn't be pushing Daisy so hard for just a pleasurable ride. But he shouted, "Colleen! Ma! Come quick, Pa's hurt!"

Colleen forgot everything she was about to say about Daisy and ran after Joey, who had already turned from the doorway and taken off again. She ran after him until she saw Daisy, breathing hard with a body slung over her back. Colleen's heart stopped at the word 'body', because this wasn't just anyone. It was Pa.

Colleen skidded to a stop a few feet away from Daisy, where Joey was trying his best to lift his pa up off the horse's back and onto his little shoulders. Colleen never knew how this little boy had ever gotten their pa up on Daisy's back to begin with. Suddenly, Colleen was in motion. Running to help her little brother, calling for her ma, and, when their ma came running, helping to carry her pa's limp body into the house.

When the three of them got him to his bed and laid him down as gently as possible, Colleen stepped back and looked at her pa. He was covered in colorful, swollen bruises, his lip was busted and his shirt and pants were torn in a few spots. Colleen knew immediately what had happened.

"Oh, Ma," Colleen whispered, looking at her mother.

"Oh my goodness!" her ma gasped, putting her hands over her mouth and flashing a terrified look at Colleen. "He's been trampled on."

Colleen looked down at her pa as silence took the room for several seconds. The other two boys suddenly appeared in the bedroom doorway. "Ma," Aaron asked. "What's wrong with Pa?" Then Colleen heard his sharp intake of air as he saw his pa. Colleen's ma moved to block their view while simultaneously telling Aaron and Riley to get out. She looked at Joey. "Keep them out of here, Joey. Colleen," her head snapped back to look at her daughter and Colleen saw tears in her mother's eyes, "Colleen, take Daisy, ride to town and get the doctor as fast as you can." Colleen was walking out the door before her ma had even finished speaking. And when she did stop, Colleen thought she heard her ma start praying that she and the doctor would make it back in time.

FOUR

That ride to town was the longest Colleen ever made. The whole way there, she kept praying the same short prayer over and over again. "God, please keep my pa alive until I get back with the doc. God, please just keep him alive." She must have said it a thousand times before she finally reached the little town and made her way to the doc's office. After repeated knocks on his door, the doctor finally opened it and said, "What's the matter, Miss Northam?"

In a hurry, Colleen told him what had happened and asked him to come quickly. The doctor nodded swiftly and said that he would. As he hitched up his team to the wagon, he kindly suggested that Colleen give her poor horse a rest and tie her up behind his office. He then asked his neighbor, the General Store owner to care for the animal until they returned. Then, they started for the Northam's ranch, the whole time Colleen wished he'd urge his team to go a little faster. They finally got there

29

after a while though, and Joey met them to take care of the doc's team as the doc rushed in the house, followed closely by Colleen, to take care of her pa.

Colleen held a fussy Abigail on her lap as she waited with her brothers for the doc's report on their pa. It seemed like hours — and perhaps it was — before the doc and their ma emerged from the room where he was. Colleen almost jumped out of her chair when she saw them.

"How is he?" she asked.

Her ma tried to smile. "He'll be alright. Lots of bruising, but he'll get better with lots of rest."

Colleen nodded.

"He won't be on his feet for a few weeks though, Mrs. Northam," the doctor said.

"I know," Colleen's ma said quietly. "I just thank God that he's alright."

The doc nodded.

"Thank you for all your help, Doc," ma said and the doctor smiled.

"I'm just glad that your Colleen, here, is as good of a rider as she is. She got to my office right quick by the looks of her horse." With a look at Colleen, he added, "I'll bring her with me tomorrow when I come to check on your pa."

"Thank you, Doctor," Colleen said.

With a tip of his hat to her ma and an encouraging smile to the rest of them, the doc walked out the door and a few minutes later they heard his wagon start back to town. Colleen helped her ma feed the hungry children and then put them to bed before they both sat down to a meal that neither of them felt like eating.

"Mama," Colleen said after a long time, "If Pa can't get up and around for another few weeks, then what are we supposed to do about the cattle? If we don't take them to the market then we won't have any money. We won't even be able to pay the doc. Much less, keep the farm."

Colleen's ma looked up from her plateful of food that she hadn't touched. "I've been thinking about that," she said slowly. "Seems to me that we'll just have to hire someone to do it for us."

"Mama, there's no one that we know who could do that for us who's not busy with their own cattle right now. And besides," Colleen ran a shaky hand over her skirt, "hiring someone would be too expensive. We couldn't do that."

"Colleen, there's no other choice," her ma said.

"There has to be. Otherwise, who could we trust with all those precious animals? There has to be another way, there—"

Colleen stopped short, an idea just now coming to her. A crazy idea. But an idea that might work nonetheless. "Ma," she said in a low voice. "I could do it."

"Colleen," ma said in an exhausted voice.

"I'm serious, Ma," Colleen said, "I could do it with the help of a few hands, just like pa. We'd leave in a few days, just like he was planning. And if I did it then we wouldn't have to worry about paying someone else. We'd make the same amount of money just like we always do."

"Colleen, don't be ridiculous," her ma said. She stood and began to clear the table. "You should know that I'd never let you do that, it's too dangerous. Besides, your pa might get better sooner than the Doc thinks and we'll just get a later start with the cattle."

"And if he doesn't?" Colleen asked.

Her ma was silent as she continued washing the dishes.

"Ma, Doc said that pa won't even be getting around for a few weeks. Who knows when he'll be able to take care of the cattle again," Colleen said. She tried to will her bottom lip to stop from trembling, but it wouldn't. She just couldn't imagine the pain her pa was probably in at this very moment. Her ma stopped washing the dishes and dried her hands on a towel. Then she walked over to Colleen and gently put her hands on her daughter's shoulders.

"God does," she said and Colleen looked up at her ma. "God knows when he'll be able to get up again. Or if he'll be able to get up again. God knows what will happen and He will provide for us, no matter what. We just have to trust Him." Colleen nodded slowly, then wrapped her arms around her ma as her ma hugged her back tightly running her hand over her daughter's straight blonde hair.

FIVE

Colleen did her best to take care of the herd in the days that followed her pa's accident. She still wasn't sure what had happened that resulted in her pa being trampled by the cattle. But cows are big animals and just the slightest thing will scare them and make them do things they wouldn't normally do. Colleen's pa had woken a few times in the last few days — once when the doc had stopped by to check on him and drop off Daisy. But if he ever told the doc or her ma what had happened, it was never mentioned to Colleen. A part of her wasn't sure if she even wanted to know. So she kept her questions to herself and took care of the herd for her pa.

Her days were so busy now that at the end of each one, Colleen could barely eat her supper and change into her night clothes before she collapsed into her bed. There was no time for her to read, although since her job now was to care for the cattle, she had plenty of opportunity to ride.

She and Joey split the chores every morning and evening, and though they didn't like it, ma had Aaron and Riley helping her in Colleen's place with all the household chores. Things started looking like they would actually be alright until one morning when Colleen woke to her ma shaking her. Suddenly, her eyes snapped open and she was awake.

"What's wrong?" she sat upright.

"It's your pa," her ma answered, "He's gotten worse. I sent Joey for the doc and they should be here soon, but I need your help with Abigail and the boys."

Colleen pulled herself, aching muscles and bones, out of bed and quickly dressed while her ma stayed with her pa. The doctor came soon after, and the bedroom door was closed for what seemed like the rest of the morning. Colleen made breakfast for herself and her younger siblings and, after taking them all out to help with the chores, the five of them sat in the house and Colleen just tried to keep them quiet.

Finally, when she was preparing the noon meal, the bedroom door opened and the doc walked out. Ma motioned to the boys and told them that pa was awake and they could see him, so the three boys walked slowly into the room. Ma walked over and took Abigail from Colleen and held her close. Colleen looked at the doctor raising her eyebrows to ask the question that her lips couldn't.

"He'll be alright now," the doctor said patting Colleen's shoulder. "When Joey came to get me this morning, I was afraid there might be some internal bleeding, but if your ma takes care of him just right, he'll be just fine. And I know Jethro's always been a good neighbor so I can almost promise that you all will be well taken care of. However, I know you've all been waiting for this time of year so your pa could take the cattle to market, but," the doc wiped a hand across his face, "I doubt your pa will be able to take those cows to market this year."

Colleen looked at her mother who just nodded, because now the doctor had confirmed what they had already feared. Colleen's ma looked upset and when she didn't say anything to the doc, Colleen looked at him and said, "Thank you for coming, Doc. We appreciate it. And don't worry, we'll get by."

The doctor smiled at her and said, "I'm sure you will." He nodded and put his hat on, then turned to leave. Colleen walked him out to his wagon and watched as he untied his team and hitched them to the wagon.

"I'll be back in a few days to check on your pa and," the doc hesitated, a frown creasing his forehead as he thought.

"And?" Colleen asked.

"And to see how the rest of you are doing," the doc answered.

Colleen didn't seem to notice how intensely the young doctor was looking at her, but she was truly grateful for all he had done to help her pa.

"Thank you," she said and she meant it with all her heart.

After the doc left, Colleen turned and went back inside to see her pa. Her brothers had started eating already by the time Colleen walked slowly into her ma and pa's bedroom and made her way around her ma's sewing machine to the bed where her pa was lying. She sat down in the chair her ma had put beside the bed and gently took his hand in both of hers. Her pa's eyes were closed when she walked in the room, but now they opened and a rusty smile came to his face when he saw Colleen.

"There's my sweet girl," her pa said in a raspy voice.

Colleen smiled and blinked the tears out of her eyes. "Hi, Pa," she whispered.

"How are you and your ma holding up?" he asked quietly because the bedroom door was still open. "She doesn't seem to want to talk about anything but me right now."

Colleen didn't know how to say how they were doing exactly, so she shrugged and said, "We'll be alright when you're alright, Pa. Everyone just needs things to go back to normal."

"Was there ever a normal for around here?" her pa asked and Colleen laughed.

"Maybe not," she said, "We just want you to get better as soon as you can."

Pa closed his eyes in understanding. "I don't know what your ma and I are going to do about the cattle," he said.

"Don't you worry about that right now, we'll take care of it," Colleen said. "You just concentrate on getting better."

"Alright," her pa said. Then after a few minutes of them sitting in silence, he said, "Oh, I'm so tired."

Colleen stood up and squeezed his hand before letting go. "You get some rest, Pa," she told him.

"Okay. I love you, Colleen," he said. She smiled back at him before walking quietly out of the room and leaning the door behind her.

SIX

Colleen leaned up against the log wall until her ma looked up from her knitting and they caught each other's gaze across the room. Colleen didn't know what they were going to do now. It was obvious that pa wouldn't be up and going for several weeks and it would be too expensive for them to hire someone and too great a burden to ask of a friend. Ma had said that she didn't want her going, because even for men it was very dangerous. Things such as heat, cattle thieves, and even wild animals made it a risky journey.

That night, after Abigail, Riley and Aaron were all in bed, Ma turned to Colleen and said, "I don't like it, but we have no other choice than for one of us to take the cattle to market."

Colleen looked at her ma in surprise. "You're actually going to let me do it?" she asked.

"I didn't say you necessarily," her ma said pointing a knitting needle at Colleen.

"I'll do it," Joey piped up from where he sat in the corner of the room, using a special kind of knife to carve a little block of wood.

"No, Joey," Ma said quietly. "People might look at me or your sister and consider us to be a small . . ." their ma heaved a heavy sigh before saying, "man . . . But you would definitely be too small," she added. "People would take advantage of your age and assume you know nothing."

Colleen and Joey looked at each other, then at their ma as it hit them, and they both blurted out at the same time, "You!"

Their ma looked at them in surprise. "Well, it has to be one of us women-folk." Then she added in a mutter, "Disgraceful!"

"Mama," Colleen said, "You have to take care of Abigail. She's just too little for me to feed her all solid food. You can't go. It'll have to be Joey or me."

"Joey's not going," their ma said firmly. After a moment, she added thoughtfully, "We could both go," and looked at Colleen.

"Uh, no, Mama," Joey said, getting up and leaving his block of wood in the corner. "Abigail?"

Ma looked down at her idle hands, despite the yarn and knitting needles in her lap. There was a long pause as they all thought. Ma thought of any way she could prevent her oldest daughter — who seemed like the only candidate for the job — from going out on such a rough road. She was bound to be found out. And everyone knew how disgraceful it was for a girl to dress up as a man. Colleen thought of how they might pull off either her or her mother for a cowboy . . . And Joey dreaded the thought that his ma and his sister might actually go together and leave him there with a baby sister, two younger brothers, and a sick pa.

Finally, their ma threw her hands up in the air and said, "Fine. If this is truly what God wants then He'll allow it to happen. If not, then He won't allow it. Like you said, Colleen, if we can't take the herd to market than we lose the farm. A man from the bank came to see me the other day about our loan on the land, and he made it very clear that if we don't pay the next bill, he'll make us leave."

Colleen looked at her ma in shock. "Why didn't you tell me this?" she asked.

"Because I didn't want you to worry. But now that it's out there, there's nothing else to do. Colleen get me some sturdy fabric and we'll make you a pair of pants that will fit better than if you wore your pa's. Tomorrow you'll have to go into town to hire some men to help you — I'd get about five or six, maybe seven, including a cook — if you're to leave when your pa planned to."

Colleen nodded seriously, wondering what to expect of the next day. There was even a part of her that was a little excited too, though she didn't dare admit it to herself.

As an afterthought, her ma said, "Remind me and I'll get you a bigger shirt in the morning."

41

"Bigger?" Colleen asked. If anything she thought she should have a slightly smaller one to keep it out of her way.

"Men . . . don't have the figures that us women folk do," her ma declared. But what she said was enough for Colleen to understand her meaning, so she just nodded her agreement while Joey looked at them both in confusion, eventually giving up trying to understand the women's talk and shaking his head.

That evening, both ma and Colleen stayed up late to make Colleen a pair of good pants. The pants were just beginning to take shape when ma sent Colleen to bed to get her rest, saying that she could finish the rest. Colleen hated leaving all the work to her ma, but it was work that needed to be done and Colleen needed her sleep before the next day, which was sure to be a long one. And she would need her wits about her for her family's sake, so she could hire good cattle hands.

SEVEN

Colleen was up and out the door in no time, the next morning. The pair of pants and a big shirt lay out for her, though there was no sign of her ma who was, on most occasions besides Christmas, the first one up in the morning. Colleen dressed hurriedly in the shirt and as strange as they felt, the pants. She pinned up her hair and added one of her pa's hats with a wide brim to the clothes she would now have to wear every day. She ate a quick breakfast, and, relying on the hope that her ma would remind Joey that he would have to do all the chores today, saddled Daisy and rode off before anyone else ever awoke. She reached Morristown in time to see the sunrise between the two green hills south of Morristown, and was ready to face the day . . . like a man, so to speak.

Right as she was making her way to the General Store, she jumped down from Daisy's back and scooped up a handful of dirt to smear across her face and chin to give her a scruffy look. Then she walked, head up, shoulders back, guiding Daisy to the General Store and tying her up where she'd have plenty of shade the whole day. Mr. Stubblefield was just unlocking his General Store when Colleen arrived, and, giving her a strange look due to the time of morning, he walked inside. The Doc responded to one farmer's "howdy" as he left his office and crossed over to the General Store, walking straight towards Colleen. Giving her a quick glance as he walked into Mr. Stubblefield's store, he said, "Good morning, sir."

In response, Colleen quickly made herself nod, touching the brim of her pa's hat; a gesture widely known among cowboys, and since that was what she was supposed to be, that's the role she must begin to play. Then she started to wonder if perhaps the reason the doc gave her such a strange look too, was because cowboys only touched their hats to ladies, not gentlemen.

"Oh, I don't know," she muttered to herself as soon as the doctor had gone inside. "This is not the person I'm supposed to be."

Finally, she forced herself to walk inside and talk — with as little eye contact as she could manage, and a really low voice — to Mr. Stubblefield about putting up a sign outside for the day advertising the reason she was there. Once he agreed, Colleen sat back and watched the little town come to life while thinking about her pa. He had to do this every year. But then it was his job. He belonged in a place like this. Colleen had never before been in town so early and was amazed by how many people were out and about during a rancher's chore time; but they were store owners, not ranchers. And just when she'd thought the nervousness had gone away, Colleen was reminded of the fact that the more people she saw, the more people she would have to try to avoid so no one would recognize her.

No one did though, and as soon as word got out that a rancher was in town looking for some cowpokes, men from all over the area who didn't have their own ranches, or were just passing through and looking for some extra cash stopped by to see if the jobs had been filled.

One of the first men who came about a job Colleen liked right away. His name was Fletcher, and although he was a serious man and Fletcher was the only name he gave, he had a certain good quality that could not be overlooked. And he seemed to Colleen to be the type of man her pa would hire, so she gave him a job and told him to go get his things ready because they would be leaving the next morning.

"Ride out to my pa's place. Mr. Northam's ranch," Colleen told him. Fletcher nodded and walked out of the General Store as a Mr. Branson, who looked vaguely familiar, walked in and sat down in front of Colleen.

"Would you be a Mr. Northam, looking for some cattle hands?" he asked her.

Colleen nodded, cleared her throat, then shrugged, "I'm Mr. Northam's son, but I'm here for the same reason," Colleen said, thankfully remembering to lower her voice. It was the hardest thing to remember about playing the part of a man.

"I worked for your father last year then," Branson said, "I came by to see if I could help out again this year. Is it his cattle we're herding?"

Colleen nodded and wrote the man's name down on a piece of paper beside Fletcher's name. "Yes, it is. I remember my pa being impressed with your work last year, Mr. Branson," she told him, then offered him her hand and hoped he wouldn't feel how soft hers was. "You've got yourself a job."

Mr. Branson shook her hand firmly and gave a small smile. He picked up his hat and held it to his chest, a thoughtful look on his face.

"What is it?" asked Colleen.

"If you don't mind my asking," Branson said, "Mr. Northam didn't have a son helping out last year. He never even mentioned having one old enough to help. Where'd you come from and what happened to him?"

Colleen cleared her throat — just like her pa did when he was nervous — and said quickly, "I rode in from out of town a few days ago. I've been gone for a while. My pa wasn't able to take the cattle market this year, so I'm doing it for him."

"Oh, alright then," Branson said and smiled again. "Welcome back."

"Thank you. I'll see you first thing tomorrow," Colleen said, and with an assuring nod, Branson left the General Store, leaving Colleen slouched in her chair, feeling bad about not being able to tell him the truth about who she really was. Maybe that was the hardest part of the job. Even over remembering to keep her voice low. She hated lying to these people.

The next man who came to talk to Colleen about getting a job, was an older man called Gus. Colleen liked him right away for the never ending list of wise things he said in just the few minutes that she talked to him. She decided that even though he was an older man, and seemed as if he could be a little cranky at times, he was just the type of man she would want on the long journey to the market. And perhaps his years of experience herding cattle would come in handy too. It wasn't long before Colleen interrupted one of Gus's many stories on cattle that he was telling her to shake his hand and tell him that he had a job. Gus smiled a big, almost toothless smile at her in thanks.

After Gus left the General Store, Colleen asked Mr. Stubblefield what time it was and he replied that it was nearing lunch time. Colleen thanked the man and was getting ready to pull out her own lunch that she'd made in a rush that morning, when another cowboy entered the General Store.

After a silent prayer over her food and for her pa back home, Colleen stuffed a bite of cold chicken in her mouth before the cowboy made his way over to her.

The day had gone well so far and Colleen had already talked to several men and had hired three. She also knew that four people — including herself — would not be enough to drive the cattle to market, and she knew in order to get more cattle hands, she would have to sit tight for a few more hours. However, at the moment, all she wanted to do was get up, walk outside, and stretch her legs. Maybe visit with Daisy a little bit before coming back inside. But as she was chewing her mouthful of food, the cowboy walked over to her and sat down in the seat across from her.

Colleen looked up at him and when she did, the food she was about to swallow almost choked her, and immediately her heart started pounding in her chest. Because the person that sat before her wasn't someone she'd never seen before, or just looked vaguely familiar, it was the young cowboy who had rescued her from the man at the fair just a few weeks ago. The one who had won the horse race. And his blue eyes pierced right through her as if he already knew who she was. Colleen forced herself to swallow her food that now felt and tasted like dirt. She knew deep in her heart that she should thank this young man for helping her because she might not ever have the chance again, but in order to do so, she would give away her disguise and give up her only opportunity to help her family and her pa. So instead of thanking him, Colleen just cleared her throat nervously again, and said, "Are you here about the job as a cattle hand?"

"I am," the cowboy said in a low voice.

"Well, there are still a few jobs left," Colleen said, barely remembering to talk lower herself. "I'm assuming you've had some experience working with cattle?" she asked.

The cowboy leaned back in his chair and said, "Yes."

Colleen raised her eyebrows. So far, she had managed to get three whole words out of him. "You must be a man of few words," Colleen let the girlish sounding words slip out then clamped her mouth shut so she wouldn't go and give herself away. She hadn't come this close to it all day.

The young cowboy just looked at her and said slowly, "I reckon you could say that."

Colleen bit her lip. Make that nine successful words. She took a breath and asked what she hoped was one of the questions her pa asked people when hiring for this occasion. "Are you from around here?"

"I lived here for a while with my folks and then I went further out west," the young cowboy said. His voice seemed to be the most grown up thing about him. As a matter of fact, he didn't seem to be much older than Colleen, although the slight frown he now wore made him look older.

"But you're back now?" Colleen asked.

"Yeah," he said. He looked as if he were distracted by something.

"Are you here to stay?" Colleen asked, reprimanding herself in her thoughts, for asking questions on her own behalf instead of on behalf of the cattle.

"I don't know that for sure yet but we'll see. A lot of it depends on this job, sir," he said.

"Please, just call me Col —" Colleen caught herself just in time "— Callen."

"That's an unusual name," the cowboy said, "I'm Danny. Daniel LaHaye. But the people I work for just call me Danny."

"Well, Mr. LaHaye," Colleen started, holding her hand out for him to shake, but he interrupted her.

"Danny," he said meeting her hand and the frown disappeared.

"Danny, then," Colleen said wondering why he was looking at her like he was. He hardly blinked and looked as if he were trying to study her . . . face! Colleen swiftly reached up to adjust her pa's hat, dearly hoping that this young man hadn't put two and two together about her face being the one he had so briefly seen at the fair that day.

"Well, Danny," she said again, "I hope you're ready to ride out tomorrow morning because that's when we're leaving."

"Thank you," he said standing up. "Mr. Northam's place, right?" he asked.

"Yes," Colleen answered, wondering how he'd guessed. Then she remembered the last name. Somehow she felt that giving him a job was enough of a thank you for now. She'd just have to say it to his face when they had made it back from the market, and her being Callen Northam didn't matter anymore.

Just as Danny was turning to leave, he stopped and looked back at Colleen. "I figured I'd see your pa here today," he said slowly. He didn't finish what he was saying, but Colleen didn't have to know him to know what he was asking.

"My pa took a stumble with some of the cattle," Colleen explained, hoping that since he'd worked as a ranch hand he would know what she meant.

"Is he okay?" Danny asked. Colleen was slightly surprised by how truly concerned he looked.

"He'll be good as new in a few weeks now that he's seen the doc," she told him. "He just needed some time to recover, so I'm here to help him out." *At least that part's true*, Colleen thought.

"Well, I'm really sorry to hear that," Danny said. "Your pa was always so kind to my folks."

"He's always kind to everybody," Colleen said and purposefully looked out the window at Daisy so that Danny wouldn't see the tears that had suddenly filled her eyes at the thought of her pa.

Seeming to sense that this was a sensitive subject, Danny put his hat on and said, "I hope he gets better real soon. He used to pay me for helping him chop wood sometimes when I was younger. When we'd get back from the woods, his little girl would ask me to swing her on the old wooden swing out by the house." Danny smiled at the memory, then seemed to remember where he was and who he was talking to; at least, who he *thought* he was talking to. "I guess his little girl would be your younger sister."

Colleen smiled uncomfortably and said, "Yes. Colleen."

She was so busy trying to act normal and not let him see how strange she felt talking to him, that she didn't notice his head jerk up after she said the name. After a moment, he said, "Well, I best be gettin' on now." With a nod to her, he turned and for a split second, Colleen caught a glimpse of his bright, almost boyish, smile and Colleen caught her breath as a memory surfaced from the very back of her mind. She was around five years old and she was a muddy mess from playing tag with a boy not much older than herself, who was equally muddy. And unless her mind was playing tricks on her, that boy sure did look a lot like Danny LaHaye. And if that was the case, then the girl he had talked about was her — giving a whole new meaning to what happened at the annual fair — and also making him highly likely to suspect that she wasn't who she said she was. Perhaps he even remembered that there was no older son in Jethro Northam's family.

Colleen tried her best to ignore the surge of emotions that were probably showing on her face. This journey was already getting too complicated, and it hadn't even started yet. Colleen pulled out her lunch that she didn't feel like eating now and the piece of paper she had been using to keep track of the men she had hired so far. She would look for just a few more men before she packed up and went home. So far she had Fletcher, Branson, Gus . . . Colleen picked up her pencil and carefully wrote on the paper: Danny LaHaye.

EIGHT

Colleen was able to hire one more cattle hand: Charles, as well as a man who claimed that his last name was actually Cooks *before* he became a cook for ranchers when they drove their cattle to market. Charles was young, but always held himself in readiness, and whenever Colleen would ask or say something that made him slightly nervous, his cheeks would turn bright red. But he showed promise as a cattle hand, in Colleen's opinion, and it was nice to know that she wouldn't be the only youngster on the trail. Leroy Cooks said he was a good jokester and an even better cook. He had the biggest smile and humorous eyes Colleen had ever seen. "Laughter and food, Mr. Northam," Cooks had told her with a laugh, "that's what keeps the men going." And as a woman, Colleen knew that nothing could lift a man's spirit better than good food, so she hired him. A part of her dreaded the trail with all these men, and having to pretend to be one herself, and yet another part of her couldn't wait to get to know them better. So with a total of six men, Colleen left town and headed home. Her ma had said six or seven men but Colleen was already feeling that six — plus herself — was just about all she could handle.

That evening, she answered all her ma's questions over supper and confirmed that she and the cattle hands would be driving the herd to market starting bright and early the next morning. Then, adding a vest to her pile of men's clothes, she went out to check the cattle to make sure that they and Daisy would be ready for the trail next morning. Colleen packed up the few possessions she would need, including a little sack of money from her ma and a family photo that could easily fit in her vest pocket. Anything she took had to be small and light, and fit in her saddle bags. She didn't want to take too much with her for fear of wearing out Daisy. So with a blanket, and a makeshift tent, a few articles of extra clothing and a bar of goat soap, Colleen tied up her little bundle and put it in her saddlebags. She assumed that was all; since they had a cook she wouldn't be needing to take food with her. A moment later, her ma walked into her room and held out a leather belt to her daughter. Colleen looked at the belt, realizing what it was, and then looked up at her ma.

"Mama," she said quietly.

"The cattle hands will expect you to have one," her ma told her, handing the gun belt and pistol to her. "They might suspect you if you don't have one."

Colleen decided as she took the gun from her ma, that now was not the time to tell her that one of the cattle hands might already suspect her.

"There should be plenty of ammunition for the trip, in the belt," her ma said as Collen put the gun and the belt with the clothes she would be wearing in the morning. "You know how to use it, right?"

Colleen nodded. "Yes, Mama."

"Well, get your sleep tonight," her ma said. "Trust me, you'll need it. Last night in a bed. I can't say that the ground's very soft at night."

Colleen nodded again, not sure what else to say. She looked at her ma. They were almost the same height now. Colleen remembered when she was little and she had to look up at her mother when she would ask her questions or tell her something. Now, here they were, almost the same height and knowing that they should be saying goodbye tonight because there would be no time in the morning, and Colleen suddenly realized that no matter how tall she was, she would always look up to her mother. Not just because her mother was a determined, strong woman, but because she had also let Colleen see her when she was weak. She had let her daughter see her be brave under terrible circumstances, and she had let her daughter see her cry. And that, to Colleen, was exactly what made her ma the most exceptional woman she knew. Colleen's ma pulled her into an embrace, holding her tightly, and whispering prayers and saying over and over again how much she would miss her and to be careful. Finally Colleen let go, assuring her ma that she would be perfectly safe. Her ma nodded and brushed the tears from her eyes with the back of her hand.

"I'm going to say goodbye to Pa," Colleen told her and turned towards her parent's bedroom.

When she walked in their small room, she saw that her pa wasn't awake, and not wanting to rouse him, she leaned over and kissed his forehead. "Goodbye, Pa," she whispered. "I love you."

Saying goodbye to Abigail Rose was hard enough for Colleen, however, her little sister wasn't old enough to ask any questions like her two brothers did. They couldn't understand why Colleen was leaving to drive the cattle to market, since that was a man's job. Colleen had also been careful not to let them see her tromping around in pants too, so that they wouldn't ask questions about that or say anything to the cattle hands in the morning, or their neighbors later on. Joey, of course, knew most of what was going on, but he also knew what not to say to the men who would be showing up in the morning. Aaron and Riley were a little harder to convince that nothing was wrong, but finally Ma came to Colleen's rescue and said that she had to do something for Pa. So eventually, Colleen was able to tell them all goodbye, and hug them tight. Then it was bedtime and Colleen laid down to sleep in her own bed, like her ma had said, for the last time until they would be back from selling the cattle. If *they made it back from selling the cattle*, Collen thought. Then she stopped and corrected herself. When *they would be back.* With God's help and protection, they would all make it back, safe and sound.

NINE

Colleen's eyes flew open the next morning and she lay still in her bed, not knowing what time it was, and wondering if her ears were playing tricks on her, or if she had really heard horse hooves outside. Then there came the sound of a man's voice from outside and Colleen jumped out of bed, changing her clothes as fast as she could without waking up her little sister whom she shared the small bedroom with. Abigail Rose stirred and Colleen froze for a moment so she wouldn't wake just yet. The second she was dressed and had pulled her hair up underneath her pa's hat, she slipped out of her room and into her ma and pa's room so she could wake up her ma and tell her that she was leaving. It would do no good to leave without telling her. Her ma woke with a start, but when she saw Colleen, in her husband's hat and clothes, she seemed to remember what today was and she got out of bed with a look of grim determination on her face.

Before Colleen could get out of the door, her ma had a breakfast of eggs, bacon, bread with butter, and coffee, and a glass of milk on the table. Colleen glanced out one of the windows and saw that Branson — who had worked for her pa the year before — was the only one who had arrived thus far, and was sitting out on the front porch smoking his pipe, in no hurry to be leaving yet. Colleen relaxed a little and finished eating her breakfast before Gus arrived and struck up a conversation with Branson.

After grabbing her saddle bags, Colleen hugged her ma one last time and held back tears for the sake of the men who would be thinking of her as their boss for the next few weeks whom she would be greeting in just a moment. Then she opened the door to the "Howdydoes" of the men outside. Just as she stepped through the doorway — her ma behind her waiting to greet the men as the lady of the house, two more men rode into the yard. With a strange kind of nervousness, Colleen saw that one of them was Danny LaHaye. He met her gaze across the yard and touched his hat. Colleen remembered that he might just know exactly who she was. So she turned and bid Branson and Gus good morning, then reached up to push her own hat more securely onto her hair. With a pointed look at Danny, she hurried off the porch and into the barn to saddle up Daisy. By the time she finished, all of the cowpokes and Cooks had arrived and were ready to start driving the cattle. With one last nod to her ma, Colleen climbed up on Daisy's back and turned her towards the field that the cattle were in.

"Be careful!" her ma called from the front porch.

And Colleen knew that her ma meant more than just the usual dangers of the trail. Adding to all those, was the fact that she was a woman. Colleen had told her ma about Branson working for her pa last year and it had helped her ma feel about as comfortable as she could in this situation. Colleen and the hands rode out to bring the cattle back and get them out onto the trail. Cooks waited for them to bring the herd on up past the house and then he fell in behind them all with his wagon full of food.

Colleen saw her brothers and her ma, holding Abigail Rose, standing out on the front porch when they led the herd past the house. She turned in her saddle to wave to them, and from a distance, she saw Danny looking over at her family wearing the same confused frown he had had the day before when she had talked to him about his family; before she had told him her name. She looked back at her family and realized that any time before now, she would have been there too, standing with them to wave goodbye to her pa. For someone who knew their family well enough, this would be enough to give the whole thing away. Colleen turned back around in her saddle and looked straight ahead. No matter what Danny or anyone else thought, she decided, she would finish what she had set out to do.

No distractions, just work, she told herself. And with that, she rode ahead to lead the cattle.

That first week spent out on the trail was one of the hardest, physically and mentally for Colleen. The first night, it was all she could do after such a long day of riding, to pull herself into her tent and take off her gun belt before falling down on the ground and going to sleep. Caring for the cattle was trying enough, but hiding the fact that she was a woman was an entirely different battle. Every time she spoke it had to be like a man; she had to walk, ride and even eat more like the men; she never had to shave which seemed to confuse the men, although they never said so. Worst of all, was the matter of her hair. Trying to keep her blonde braids under her hat was a minute by minute task, and she feared that at any point, the wind would whip her hat right off her head and give her away.

Her hair wasn't the only thing that troubled her either. Her back hurt constantly from riding so much throughout the day, and sleeping on the ground made it no better. What's more, is she wasn't nearly as strong or tall as the men and more than a few times, she had to call one of the hands over to help her wrestle a cow back into line. Physically, she wasn't able to do the job. Night was a big relief from the day's back-breaking work, but with it was the questioning looks from her hired hands who slept out under the stars every night, whereas Colleen chose to sleep in the small tent she had brought with her in her saddle bags. She would have actually liked to have slept out under the stars too, but she couldn't very well sleep with a hat on. And when the rain started, she had a good reason to be thankful for her little tent.

However, once the rain started, it didn't stop. It had been cloudy the day before and then that night it opened up and poured all night. Colleen knew it was dangerous for the herd to be trudging along the rocky, slippery slopes here and there, and more than once a cow, or cowboy and his horse, almost went down, but luckily there were no injuries during that first day. That night, they sat around a campfire that sputtered despite the two blankets that were hung over sticks stuck into the muddy earth to protect the flames. Cooks served them all hot coffee and hot food that warmed them and lifted their spirits some, and Colleen wondered how he ever managed to get it all hot. But talk still eventually turned to letting the rain pass by them before moving on again.

"If we don't keep going, we won't make it to market on time," Colleen said shivering despite the blanket around her shoulders.

"If we keep going we'll run the chance of hurting ourselves or the cattle," Fletcher said.

"Nah, I've ridden through worse, with the boys," Gus said waving his hand and almost blowing the out the sputtering campfire flames with the gesture.

The other men, especially Cooks who had worked so hard to get it going, scolded him for it, but Colleen just smiled. Gus always called any cattle hands he'd worked with previously 'the boys'. She wondered if after this, and if they didn't find out about her, she would someday be in that group of his. Maybe bosses weren't included, she wasn't sure.

"Bad as a bunch of old women," he muttered, referring to the campfire.

Colleen looked down at her lap.

Cooks poured them all a second cup of hot coffee and Colleen turned to look in the direction of the herd. Danny had gone out to check them one last time before they all settled down for the night, and had not yet returned.

"Danny not back yet?" Cooks asked her when he had seen the forgotten coffee cup sitting on the ground where Danny had been. Colleen turned back to the campfire and shook her head. "I'll wait to pour his coffee until he gets back then," Cooks said and returned the kettle to the campfire before sitting back down again.

"It's too bad someone don't have an instrument to play us some tunes on," Branson said.

"Ah! I could go for that," Charles said, a smile crossing his face.

He was handsome already but when he smiled, Colleen decided, he looked more handsome, and a little mischievous. Charles wasn't much older than her either, she had found out. He was the big brother of a large

64

family with twelve children, and out of all the hands he seemed to be the only one who was willing to share family memories and stories with Colleen. She found herself getting attached to all the men actually; Cooks was like the kind uncle who helped you smile on rough days . . . Gus would be the grandfatherly figure, mostly just because of his age and the laid back way he looked at life . . . Fletcher didn't remind Colleen so much of a family member, but possibly a really good friend . . . Branson was the cousin figure and Charles was the sweet older brother who made you laugh, even when you didn't want to. When it came to Danny LaHaye through, Colleen wasn't too sure what part he played, but recently he seemed to be more of a boss than she was. Otherwise, they were like one big happy, soaked family.

Colleen turned her head at the sound of approaching footsteps and breathed a sigh of relief when she saw Danny walking towards them, drenched through with rain. He sat down beside her wearily, taking off his hat and letting the water the brim had collected pour off onto the ground.

"Were they okay?" she asked him.

A quick nod answered her question.

"So what do you think?" she asked.

Finally, he turned to her. "What do you mean?" he asked.

"Do you think we can keep on going tomorrow?" she asked.

Danny shrugged and turned to stare into the fire. "I say we sit tight and wait to see what tomorrow brings," he said. "We can decide what to do in the morning."

Colleen nodded in agreement and listened as their whole camp fell silent. The only sound to be heard now was the steady fall of the rain beating at the small blankets above their heads.

"It's going to be a long night," Fletcher said indicating the rain.

"I don't miss the mosquitoes though," Charles said. It was true, the mosquitoes on the trail were consistent pests. They had thankfully disappeared for the most part since the rain had started, but the itching from their bites hadn't.

"I think we should all try to sleep here under the blankets," Gus said.

"I've got my tent," Colleen said, "I'll be dry enough in there and it will give you guys some more room if you choose to stay under here."

"The ground will be wet," Gus warned.

"I'm figuring if this rain keeps up everything that's not wet now, will be soon," Colleen said.

"That's true," Cooks said pointing at her.

The men started scooting in closer to the fire and Colleen couldn't help but wish she had brought a bible with her. She could have read to the men. Of course if she had brought one with her, it would be drenched too and it would be ruined. Still, she knew some verses by heart, so for the next few minutes that the men were setting in, she silently quoted some scriptures from memory. When the men's chatter had died down, Colleen noticed that Danny hadn't moved yet. He was still hunched in the same position he had been. When she looked at him, he almost immediately returned the glance. He wore the same frown he had the morning they left. So Colleen plucked up her courage and asked, "Is something troublin' ya?"

"Just thinkin'," he said.

With the rain pouring around them and the fire crackling, it was easier for Colleen to talk a little more like herself without it being too noticeable.

"About what?" she asked.

"I didn't see your sister when we left with the cattle," Danny said in a quiet voice.

Colleen hadn't expected him to say anything about that, or at least not now. And she wasn't really sure if this was a play to get her to talk, or if it's what he had really been thinking about. Maybe it was both.

"Abigail? I guess . . . I didn't pay attention," Colleen evaded.

"No, Colleen . . . Is she married?" Danny asked.

Colleen looked at him. How could she ever answer that question without giving herself away? Or was that he what he wanted?

He seemed to suspect that this was a sensitive subject so he said, "I left town for several years. Seems like now that I've come back, all the people I knew as a kid are all growin' up and gettin' married."

Colleen wasn't sure who he had known as a child, but it was true that quite a few of the young men and women in Morristown had recently gotten married. And there were two more weddings planned in spring. And if Ellie Hollister could get her way, she and Arnie McCaslin would be next.

Colleen cleared her throat. "She's not married," she answered.

Danny threw a small rock at the fire and bowed his head as he said, "I bet."

Colleen watched him, choosing her words carefully. Finally, she said in her best threatening voice, "Hey, that's my sister you're talking about."

Danny surprised her when he smiled. "Is it?" he asked softly. He almost sounded as if he were trying not to laugh.

Colleen glanced at the other hands who were oblivious to their conversation. Then she looked back at Danny, confused as to why she was actually angry with him. But when she looked into his blue eyes, she suddenly realized why. Everything in his face told her something she had worried about many times before. Once again, his frown was gone, but in its place was the realization of who she really was. He knew! Danny knew who she was and could reveal the truth to all the hands at any time. Even though for now he made no move to do so. Colleen was furious. With him for realizing it, with herself for not being more careful, and with the cattle for hurting her pa to begin with.

Angry tears threatened to spill over Colleen's eyelids but she wouldn't let Danny LaHaye see her cry, so she stood up, almost upsetting the blankets over their heads, and stomped out into the rain to set up her tent. If he wanted to tell the other hands, fine. She had no attachment to him. She would end his job the next opportunity she got, whether she had thanked him for saving her at the fair, or not.

TEN

The next morning was just as wet and depressing as the day before. Colleen and the hands woke up and decided after much debate that they could only keep going. The rain could end at any moment or it could continue on until they reached the end of their journey. But it would do no good to sit and try to wait it out. They would just keep their heads down and ride out the storm. Colleen was especially in favor of this option, due to the fact that it would get her away from Danny LaHaye quicker, and in her opinion, the sooner they reached the next town and she could tell him his services were no longer required, the better. And she made certain to stay clear of him during breakfast, even though she stole glances at him to see if he was watching her. Most of the time he wasn't.

She sat by Charles and Cooks as they ate their breakfast of biscuits, bacon and dried fruit. Before she began eating, Colleen closed her eyes and said a silent prayer for the food and her and the hands as well as the cattle. She made herself also pray for a truce of sorts, between herself and Danny. Then silently, she begged in her prayer, "God, please don't let him give me away. I hate having to deceive them all, they're good men, but I have to help my pa and I have no other way to do so. So if it's Your will, let him not ruin all the hard work that's been put into this. And please, God, help my pa. Heal him, and be with my family. Thank you, God, for Your blessings. Amen." When Colleen looked up, taking a bite of her biscuit, she noticed Charles staring at her, a curious expression on his face. *Oh no*, she thought, *not him too*. But his question had nothing to do with her particularly.

"Boss, were you just prayin'?" he asked.

Colleen swallowed her food and nodded. She still wasn't used to being called Boss.

"Why do you pray?" Charles asked his cheeks bright red.

Colleen put down her biscuit and thought for a moment before answering, "Well, I pray because it's a way for me to talk to God."

"Can anyone talk to God?" he asked.

"Yes, of course," she answered.

Charles looked down at his hands and untouched food, probably aware of all the other hands looking at him, wondering where this was going. Colleen wondered that herself, although she tried not to let it show on her face. Without looking at Colleen, Charles said, "My family always has gone to church, but I'm afraid I never paid much attention."

He paused, then looked up at Colleen. "Will you pray with me, Boss?" he asked.

His request shocked even Colleen. She had been prepared to ride with a bunch of men and act like one herself in order to get by. Not once did she ever think about the possibility of sharing her religion with them. And especially to be asked by one of the men to do it. The idea excited her in a way she couldn't put into words.

"Yes. Yes, I'll pray with you," she said. "Right now?"

Charles nodded.

She reached out her hand and he grabbed it with his own big hand. Before she could begin, Cooks reached over and took her other hand in his.

"Pray with us all, if you don't mind . . . Sir," he said.

As he spoke, Colleen watched all the other men grab each other's hands forming a circle, started by Cooks and quickly followed by Danny. Colleen smiled and nodded at Cooks. Then she closed her eyes and, almost forgetting to lower her voice, began.

"Dear Father, even though it's raining, we thank You for this glorious day," she prayed. "And as I prayed earlier, please bless this day, bless the food and all of these hardworking men. Help us all to realize that we are Yours and that everything we do is a blessing from You. This rain is a blessing. Lord, we ask that Your will be done. That You show us what is the right way, where You want us to go. We all have trials that we are facing, have faced, or will face. God, please help us through those. And not only that we get through those, but that we come out on the other side, praising Your name, no matter the outcome. Father, I also think that You are calling some of the people right here, to You. And Lord I pray that they find their way and that You touch their hearts and open their eyes to You. Lord, please bless Charles, Cooks, Fletcher, Danny, Gus, and Branson . . . Amen."

Colleen opened her eyes, almost expecting to see the sun shining because of the way she felt, but it was still raining. Everyone slowly let go of each other's hands and Colleen savored the moment. She felt a little like a preacher after a good long sermon. That prayer had been a powerful one, she knew. Even though she hadn't started it out with that in mind. Of course, lots of things so far had turned out differently from what she imagined. Charles interrupted her thoughts when he stood up so suddenly that he bumped the blankets hanging over their heads to keep the rain off, and a stream of water gushed in.

"Sorry, sorry," he stammered, trying to fix it, but only making it worse. Danny jumped up and helped him pull the blanket back over them but by that time, Colleen had been doused in icy cold water. "Sorry, Boss," Charles said looking at her.

Colleen waved him off as she readjusted her hat, willing herself not to shiver or she'd make poor Charles feel even worse.

"It's fine," she said, forcing a laugh through her chattering teeth.

"Could I have a minute, Boss?" Charles asked. "I'm not real hungry, but I appreciate the breakfast, Cooks."

Cooks nodded and Colleen smiled. "You go ahead, Charles," she told him.

With an excited bounce in his step, Charles put on his hat, grabbed his coat and started out into the rain. "I'll check the cattle too," he said over his shoulder. He disappeared into the rain in just a few seconds.

"You know, sir," Cooks said thoughtfully to Colleen, "I think you might just be changin' that young man's life."

Colleen smiled.

"No, that wouldn't be me."

"What's he thinking," Fletcher said, "He'll get pneumonia if he stays wet all day." He started to get up but Colleen reached out and touched his arm.

"No," she said barely audible over the drumming rain, "Let him go."

"But, Boss," Fletcher said in a confused sounding voice.

"He'll be fine," Colleen assured him, then shivered visibly.

"Here," Danny said taking his own blanket and wrapping it around her shoulders.

"I'm fine," she said trying to give the blanket back.

But Danny refused.

"No, take it," he said. "You're the boss."

He helped her reposition the blanket back on her shoulders, then sat down beside her. She looked at him for a long time trying to figure him out. Danny looked out at the rain in the same direction Charlie had gone. Once again, he could have revealed the truth to the other men, and Colleen wasn't quite sure why he didn't. Instead, he chose to help her. Could it be possible, she thought, would he actually not tell anyone? She had never thought about that before. She had always assumed he would tell the other men because she figured he'd think it was the right thing to do. And maybe he was still trying to find the right time, but for the first time during their journey so far, Colleen felt something for Danny LaHaye besides frustration. Now, she was feeling appreciation. Appreciation for the fact that he hadn't said anything about her to the other men, and appreciation for the idea of him not necessarily being a tattle-tale.

When Danny looked away from the rain and over at her, she quickly looked away not wanting to show her feelings in her eyes. The day they bid each other farewell once and for all, perhaps she would be able to find it in her to thank him for all he had done for her, including the incident back at the fair. Because then she would be able to thank him honestly as Colleen.

"Well, we'd better get going if we're planning on getting those cows anywhere today," Gus said standing up.

"Yes, let's be on our way," Colleen said doing the same.

Charles came back as they were packing up the last bits of what made up their camp, and asked to speak with Colleen alone. When they had walked around to the other side of the covered wagon, Charles could contain his excitement no longer.

"Boss, you were right," Charles said and Coleen wondered if he wasn't trying to keep himself from jumping up and down as he talked.

"What do you mean?" Colleen asked.

"Anyone can talk to God," Charles answered excitedly, "And I found Him."

Colleen felt like it no longer mattered how many buckets of water were being poured on their heads now. Her eyes lit up and a huge smile spread across her face as she realized what he meant.

"Oh, Charles, that's wonderful!" she exclaimed. Before she knew exactly what she was doing, Colleen had reached up and thrown her arms around his neck to hug him. Perhaps an actual boss on these trails wouldn't do such a thing, but at the moment Colleen didn't really care. Silently, she thanked God for leading this young man right. She was sure Charles was headed for a good life.

The trail was rough and muddy and the rain blew right into Colleen's face, stinging her cheeks. She had never been so afraid that her hat would blow off either. She had just recovered from a slip that could have resulted in a bad fall for both her and Daisy, when she heard a shout, somewhere to her right and a little behind her. Colleen turned in her saddle, despite the force of the rain in her face, to see if she could see who it was. But with the sheets of rain pouring down, she couldn't see much beyond Daisy's neck. Whoever it was that had shouted was mixed up in the herd though, that much she could tell . . . Another shout came, closer this time, and it wasn't so much a shout as it was a cry for help. Colleen turned Daisy into the herd, and hurriedly they worked their way through the wet cattle, towards where it sounded like the shout came from.

"Who's over here?" Colleen shouted as loud as she could to be heard over the cows and the rain.

"Gus? Branson?" she called.

There was no answer, but before she could yell out again, she saw something through the rain. A figure lying on the ground with a horse laying on top of him. Colleen made Daisy move through the crowded cattle towards whoever the person was, a sick feeling in her stomach. Then she saw who it was on the ground. "Charles!" she yelled, jumping to the ground and almost being hit by one of the cow's heads. She ran towards him, her feet slipping in the mud, trying not to disturb the cattle in the process. When she reached Charles and knelt beside him, she saw blood all over the ground around him.

"Charles," she said reaching up with shaky hands to touch his face. He didn't respond to her voice or her touch. His horse lay on top of him, trying to get to its feet. Behind her, Colleen heard a horse whinny and when she looked up, she saw Danny jump down and run over to her. First, he tried to get Charles's horse off of him. And finally, after a lot of encouraging words to the horse, he was able to pull it off of Charles, but he still couldn't get it to stand.

Danny came over to Colleen and looked at Charles. He put his head down to Charles' chest, just above his heart, and listened carefully. After an awful moment, with Colleen thinking of her pa's own accident, Danny raised his head and gripped Colleen's shoulder to the point of pain. Slowly, painfully, Danny shook his head and Colleen's heart sank. The trembling in her hands stopped, but that's when the tears started. Charles, so young and innocent and handsome; who had just come to know the Lord. Whose cheeks turned red when he was nervous, whose whole life was ahead of him . . . what would his family say, when they heard the news. Colleen looked away as the rain mixed with her tears. One of the other hands rode up, and somehow the cattle knew to stop and wait for them, or perhaps they were too miserable to keep going in all this rain.

Colleen stood up and backed away from the body as Fletcher and Gus both jumped down from their horses and asked Danny what happened -- which, of course, Danny could only guess himself. There had been a big rock down by Charles. The only thing Colleen could think of was that his horse had slipped in the mud and had fallen and Charles had it the rock. Colleen grabbed Daisy's reins and led her away from the men and the body. As she walked, there was a muffled gunshot, and Colleen knew it was for Charles's horse. The cattle lowed and moved away from the sound, but Gus rode past her to keep them all in line. For a moment, Colleen had the fleeting thought that they might stampede, but she knew that these cowboys had everything under control even if she didn't. So Colleen just kept walking, unable to do anything to stop herself.

ELEVEN

They made camp not long after that night, and Colleen made an effort to avoid everyone especially Danny, who seemed to want to talk to her. The next morning, the rain had stopped. Colleen woke later than usual, due to fatigue and due to the fact that she couldn't sleep after what happened to Charles. She couldn't help but feel responsible. For one, it had been her he was working for, and two, she had been the one who had made the decision to keep going, even in all the rain.

After a subdued breakfast, Danny and Branson went out to dig a grave, and Gus helped them bury Charles before all six of them gathered around the grave. Then they all stood there until Fletcher finally spoke up, "Someone should say a few words for the lad." They all agreed, but then they all turned to look at Colleen. She wasn't sure why until she remembered that she was supposed to be the boss. So she cleared her throat and opened her mouth without thinking of what she should say. The words that came out were from the Bible, and she somehow felt it would've been the exact thing young Charles would have wanted her to say in his honor. So she quoted from memory Psalm 23.

"'The Lord is my shepherd; I shall not want. He maketh me to lie down in green pastures' He leadeth me beside the still waters. He restoreth my soul: He leadeth me in the paths of righteousness for His name's sake. Yeah, though I walk through the valley of the shadow of death, I will fear no evil: for Thou art with me; Thy rod and Thy staff they comfort me. Thou preparest a table before me in the presence of mine enemies: Thou anointest my head in oil; my cup runneth over. Surely goodness and mercy shall follow me all the days of my life: and I will dwell in the house of the Lord for ever.' Amen."

Colleen realized when she had finished that she hadn't really done anything to change her voice, but no one made mention of it so she ignored it too. The hands went back to the covered wagon to help Cooks get lunch ready, for something to do. Colleen stayed where she was though and waited until they were gone to kneel down and touch the soft mound of earth before her.

"I'm sorry, Charles," she said. "Sometimes God's plans . . . aren't meant for us to understand them. And I'm terribly sorry that this happened to you. I'm sorry."

Colleen stood and turned around, then stopped in her tracks. Danny stood a few feet away, not close enough to hear, but close enough to still be present. He slowly walked toward her. When he got to the grave where she was standing, he took off his hat, revealing dark brown, wind blown hair, and he looked deep into her eyes.

"We should talk," he said.

"Not now," she told him then started forward but ended up right in front of him. She suddenly felt dizzy, so she reached up and grabbed his shoulders, squeezing his shirt between her fingers for something to hang on to.

She had already decided what she was going to do. She would write a letter to her family explaining what happened and then tell them that she wouldn't be able to finish the job. She would tell them she was sorry and that she loved them, and then she would never go home again. Maybe she would go west. Or east. It didn't really matter anymore. She would mail the letter in the next town they stopped at for supplies and be done with it. If Gus or any of the other hands wanted to take the cattle on to market, then she would only ask that they give some of the money to her folks when they got back. However, before she got to writing the letter, she would have to make herself walk away from Danny. She let go of his shoulders and let her hands drop down to her sides before she met his demanding gaze.

"Don't you think it's time you tell me the truth?" he asked, then, lowering his voice, he added, "Colleen."

Colleen squeezed her eyes closed, then opened them slowly.

"You already know," she whispered.

"Not all of it," he said. "I don't know why your pa would let his oldest daughter dress as a man, instead of comin' out here himself. All I know is that you don't know what you're doing out here. You need my help. And whatever's going on with your family, it must have been really important for your pa to let you come out here, or . . . he didn't know."

"You know the important thing," she said. "I'm out here. And I don't know what I'm doing." Then when he kept waiting, she went on. "My pa . . . may or may not know I'm out here, but it's not his fault. My pa had an accident when he was out with the cattle, I still don't know exactly what happened, other than the fact that he was trampled. There is no way that he would have been able to drive the cattle to market, and my brother Joey is too young, so it was either me or my ma who had to do it, and I knew she couldn't leave with the baby or the boys." Colleen looked steadily at Danny. "If I hadn't come out here, my family wouldn't have been able to stay on our ranch."

"And after all that, you're still willing to just give up," Danny said.

It wasn't even a question. Colleen wasn't sure how he had read her thoughts but he had voiced exactly what they were.

In answer to her questioning look, Danny simply said, "I've seen that look before. I haven't been a ranch hand for several years and not seen people give up."

"What else am I supposed to do?" Colleen asked.

"You finish what you came out here to do," Danny answered. "Because that's the girl I knew when we were both little."

"Yeah, but how?" Colleen asked. She couldn't really see any other way than giving up.

"Because 'I can do all things . . .'" Danny started, reminding Colleen that even though she felt alone out here on the open prairie, God was still with her, and she felt comforted.

"'. . . Through Christ which strengtheneth me,'" she finished.

"That's right," Danny said. "And I'll help you too."

Colleen forced a smile.

"Thank you," she said, "I needed to remember that."

There was a pause before Danny spoke again.

"Accidents happen," he said, "People die all the time out here on the trail, so don't blame yourself. What happened to Charles was not your fault."

"That doesn't stop someone from feeling like it was their fault though," she told him.

"It wasn't your fault," Danny said again, his blue eyes staring intensely into her own.

Colleen couldn't look at Danny so she looked away, but she nodded to show she understood. Or at least she was trying to.

"Come on," Danny said and turned back towards the covered wagon. "Cooks is probably waiting for us."

Colleen started to follow him, then stopped.

"Danny."

He turned around to look at her, his face showing concern.

"You won't tell them about me, will you?" she asked.

Danny looked down and then back up at her with a small smile playing across his face. "Don't you worry about that," he said.

This time, Colleen didn't have to make herself smile. It came naturally.

TWELVE

In honor of Charles, Colleen told everyone they would stay put for the rest of the day. And since it was so muddy, none of the hands objected to the rest. Colleen also remembered that it was Sunday, and spent some time going through some of the scriptures she knew in her head. Later on, Danny pulled Colleen aside and mentioned something about her hair. She wasn't sure what he meant until she reached up and felt that the tip of her braid was falling out from underneath her pa's hat. Quickly she stuffed it back up under the brim before anyone else could see it, but Danny still frowned at it.

"We need to fix that," he said.

"What do you mean? How can I fix it?" Colleen asked.

Danny thought for a second and then, reaching into his pocket, he pulled out a small knife. Colleen looked at him, her eyes wide, and he just shrugged. "It would be a whole lot easier than trying to keep it all stuffed under that hat," he explained.

Colleen sighed. She knew he was right. Slowly, she turned around and checked to make sure that no one was coming, then, reaching up, she pulled off her hat and let her dirty hair fall out of its braid. Then, closing her eyes, she let Danny saw through her blonde hair, chopping off her beautiful locks.

Once he had finished, her head felt oddly light and she lifted a shaky hand to feel what was left of her hair. Tearfully, she realized that Danny had cut it until it was shoulder length. Colleen dug a small hole in the ground with her hands and buried her hair so that no-one would find it and suspect her. Then, avoiding Danny's attentive eyes, she quickly made her way to her tent and cried because of her missing hair, and her good friend, both of whom she would have to leave behind her when they left. However, when Colleen was ready to emerge from her tent again, she found it was a lot easier to pull the short, blonde waves up under her hat, than it was before when her hair was down to her waist.

That night they all enjoyed some cornbread biscuits that Cooks made, and that night they all sat around the fire with a bowl of cooked beans for supper. Danny sat by Colleen for both meals, but instead of making her feel uncomfortable or frustrating her, him being there made her remember that not all hope was lost, and that, now that the truth was out — no taking it back — he would be there to help her. He also kept his word and, to Colleen's relief, the hands didn't assume anything at all.

As they sat under the twinkling stars — that had never looked so pretty to Colleen before the rain — Colleen found how strange it was to think how just the other night, she was determined to do without Danny LaHaye. Now it pained her to think what she might have done without him. Then she remembered that when they got back to Morristown, and she went home, she wouldn't be seeing him every day, and she might not ever see him again once they said goodbye at the end of their journey. She would have to do without him then . . . Danny laughed at something Branson said and Colleen pushed the thought away. If she had to do without him, then she would figure out how when the time came. Until then, she would enjoy the time they spent together.

They left their little campsite early the next morning. As they drove the cattle toward the next town: Ellington, Colleen looked back at Charles' grave and whispered her thanks and goodbye to the young man. Gus had made a little grave marker for him out of wood yesterday; it had his name and the year carved into the small cross. With one last backwards glance, Colleen turned Daisy toward Ellington and helped keep the cattle moving West. They reached Ellington the next morning and stopped the herd just outside the little town. While Gus and Colleen went in to buy supplies and some extra food items for Cooks, the rest of the men stayed with the herd, and Colleen left Danny and Gus in charge. While she and Gus quickly gathered supplies at the General Store, a man from the telegraph office came in and walked up to Gus.

"Would you be a Mr. Northam?" he asked.

Gus turned and pointed to Colleen. "I'm not, but he is," he said.

The man turned to Colleen and held out a note. "Then this will be for you," he told her.

Colleen reached out and took the telegram from him. Her heart beat against her chest as she quickly read the message. It was from home. It said: PA BETTER AND WONDERING ABOUT YOU STOP WE LOVE YOU. Colleen blinked back tears as she read the message over and over again, memorizing this little piece of news from home. *Oh, thank you, God! Thank you, Lord!* Finally, Colleen looked up from the telegram and said, "I'd like to respond to this if there's a way for me to."

The man who had brought the message nodded. "Of course. It's only a few cents to send a ten word telegram. I'll show you the way to my office, if you'd like," he offered.

Colleen nodded eagerly, wondering what about the journey so far, she could say in ten words. She turned to Gus. "If you wouldn't mind finishing up here and I'll meet you back out of town," she said.

Gus agreed and so she left him in the General store and followed the man to the telegraph office. He told her on the way, that a few days ago they had received a message about the one he'd given to Colleen, saying that it was for a rancher by the name of Northam who should be passing through in a few days. So he personally had checked with all of the ranchers passing through to see if one of them had the name of Northam. "Of course, until you came, none of them did," he said, "But plenty of them reported having seen enough rain for a year, so I figured you might have been caught out in it too. Did you experience such troubles?" he asked as they reached his office.

Colleen looked around her at the telegraph office. There were drawers and files everywhere and a big map was pinned to one of the walls. An oil lamp hung from the ceiling and on a desk was the telegram machine.

"I saw my share of rain," Colleen said in a low voice. "Lost one of my men to it."

"Oh, I'm sorry to hear that," the man said. "Perhaps you would like to send a telegram to his family also?"

Colleen stopped in her tracks. The man was probably just trying to get her to pay more money for another telegram, but it was true. It was only right for Charles' family to know, but she didn't even know his last name. And she wasn't sure she had enough money for two. Finally, she decided to include that message in the one to her family, and then they could find Charles' family and pass the message on to them.

Colleen swallowed hard. "I think I'll just stick with the one," she said.

The man nodded and told her that it would be twenty cents for a ten word telegram. At that, Colleen knew she'd made the right decision to send just one telegram. If it cost that much, then one telegram would definitely have to be enough. She only had a few extra dollars that her ma had given her before she left, and she was trying to spend as little of that as possible. Finally, she decided on what she should say; her message read: ALL IS WELL STOP MISHAP WITH CHARLES STOP CONDOLENCES. Colleen paid the man, then turned, still clutching the one from home in her hand, as she walked out, and the man began the process of sending her message to her family.

Colleen rode back out to the herd and gave the call to move out. It was nearing evening already but they could cover at least another mile before they stopped for the night. The dust nearly choked Colleen as they got the herd moving again. She couldn't believe that with all the rain they had traveled through, it had apparently never reached Ellington. The little town had just disappeared into the prairie behind them when Danny suddenly rode up beside her.

"There are about five men who have been following us ever since we left Ellington," he told her calmly. "Probably rustlers."

Colleen looked where Danny gestured and saw five men on horseback just watching them from a distance.

She looked at Danny. "What should we do?"

"It's hard to tell with them," he said, "All rustlers are different, but it might be best just to ignore them."

"Then shouldn't we not let them see us looking at them?" she asked.

"No, it's good that they see us looking at them," Danny said, "It means that we're not to be challenged because we know they're up there."

"You've encountered them before?" Colleen asked nervously.

"Not *them*," Danny answered, "but men like them."

"So should we stop and make camp here, for the night?" she asked. "We'd be closer to a town if we need one."

"True, but now that they know we've seen them," Danny said, "It'll put them off for a little while."

"And then what?" Colleen asked.

"Then we keep on our way and leave it up to them. If they think they can risk it, more than likely they'll try it when we're not prepared," he said.

"So . . ." Colleen wasn't sure what he meant, and was trying to get him to tell her his whole plan.

"So we should tell the men to be on the lookout," Danny said, "As long as we're prepared, then they shouldn't try anything."

"Shouldn't?" Colleen said and looked at him doubtfully.

"Let's just say they're unpredictable. You know how to shoot, right?" Danny asked nodding to the gun holstered at her side.

Colleen had all but forgotten about that means of protection. Every day she had put on the belt and tied it down on her leg, giving no thought to actually having to use it, although it was there if she ever had need of it. She shuddered at just the thought of taking someone's life. Although she was sure that if it came down to it, and she had to, then she would. But she hoped and prayed that she would never have to use it on this journey.

She shrugged turning back to Danny. "Yes, but I don't plan on having to."

"No one usually does. But you'll use it if they decide to make a move on your pa's cattle," Danny said.

"My pa says that one human life is more important than all those cattle combined," Colleen said.

"That's true, and I'm not trying to argue, but," Danny smiled slightly, in a way that Colleen wasn't sure she liked, "after these next few days, I have a feeling you'll be seeing a little more of the trail, and be using that gun of yours, a little more than you'd like to."

Colleen smiled back. "We'll see," was all she said.

Danny tipped his hat to her and rode towards the front of the herd. Colleen shook her head. She wasn't always too sure of that Danny LaHaye. Maybe someday she would figure him out. In the meantime, though, she knew it was her job as the boss to keep a careful eye on that bunch of rustlers, as Danny had called them.

The men on horseback made no movement toward the cattle or any of the hands though, and eventually they disappeared behind a hill. Colleen wasn't sure what made her more uncomfortable: being able to see them, or not knowing where they had disappeared to. Colleen let the herd go on for another mile, hoping to put some distance between them and the rustlers, and also hoping to make up some of the time they lost during the rain, and the day they took off from traveling. Eventually though, she and the hands were hot and tired and the cows kept moving slower and slower, so she called to the hands and they all settled in for the night. After Cooks made them some supper and they all drank their fill of water after such a hot day, the hands laid down by the campfire and Colleen set up her little tent between them and the covered wagon. She was just taking off her coat and hat to lay down and fall asleep when she heard a low rumble. She sat up and listened intently, now hearing that the men were moving about too.

She heard hooves, and then she was on her feet, pulling her coat back on and tucking her hair, that she had just taken out of its short braid moments ago, back up under her hat. She was out of her tent in no time, but no time was already too late. Three men had already surrounded the hands and Cooks, making them kneel on the ground, and two more were just jumping down from their horses. They looked like they were in charge. And Colleen recognized the bunch as the men — the rustlers — who had been watching them earlier in the day. The first one saw Colleen and started toward her at the same time that Danny jumped up from his knees to try to reach her, but the second man shot right between Danny's feet and yelled at him to stay back. Colleen shot Danny a terrified look as the words he'd said earlier, *"As long as we're prepared, then they shouldn't try anything,"* echoed in her head. She looked down at her leg, realizing that she had already taken her gun belt off for the night and her gun lay back in the tent, completely useless.

The first rustler grabbed her shoulder with a heavy hand, that in a scary way seemed familiar. She suddenly thought that she could smell baked goods like towns always had at . . . and then it hit her . . . Fairs! This man was the same man who had sought her out at the fair. Then, with a sickening feeling, she wondered that if it was so easy for her to recognize him, would he just as easily be able to recognize her, in her cowboy's clothes? The man pushed her roughly towards the hands without another thought, and as she fell in with the group she saw Danny take a small step back. At least they hadn't singled her out.

The second man turned to them and asked, as he casually swung his gun past their faces, "Who's in charge of this, here, herd?"

Before Colleen could open her mouth, Danny reached over and grabbed her wrist, squeezing it so hard it hurt. Colleen took her cue from him not to say anything but she did wish he wouldn't squeeze her wrist so hard. Finally, he let go.

"I said, who's in charge?" the man demanded. He lifted his gun and aimed it right at Colleen. She knew she was the youngest and the man was trying to play on the sympathies of whoever was the boss. When again no one answered, the man laughed and lowered his gun. Then he looked at Danny.

"Well, I guess I'll just take my pick, then," he said and reached out and grabbed Danny's arm, pulling him forwards and aiming his gun at Danny's back.

"No!" Colleen shouted and started toward them, but the man from the fair grabbed her shirt collar in one fist and her arm in his other, keeping her from going anywhere. Colleen tried to avoid making eye contact with the man, but he saw into her face before she could turn away.

"Do I know you?" he asked and Colleen winced at the smell of whiskey on his breath and the fact that her pa wasn't there, and Danny wasn't able to save the day this time. She refused to answer the man.

The man who was holding onto Danny glanced back at the two of them. "Hey, bring the boy too," he told the man from the fair. "He could be a good addition to our group."

"Alright, enough," Danny spoke up, looking his captor in the eye.

"So you are the boss," the man said, smirking.

Colleen looked over at Danny, now more concerned for his safety than she was for her own, or the hands'.

"Bring the boy, Dooley," the man said without looking away from Danny. The man from the fair: Dooley, pushed Colleen forward and she kept her eyes on the ground.

"Ready when you are, Mason," Dooley said.

"You three stay with the cowpokes," Mason said, using his gun to gesture to the hands.

Colleen looked over at the four of them being held at gunpoint by the other three rustlers, and was sorry she'd ever gotten them into this situation. Granted, it wasn't her fault, but since she was the said owner of the cattle, she felt responsible. Branson caught her eye and it looked as if he was trying to tell her something with his eyes, but Dooley and Mason made her and Danny start walking away from the rest of them, and she didn't quite understand what he was trying to tell her. Colleen walked behind Danny, watching his boots, almost oblivious to any other feeling besides the cold gun barrel in her back. They walked for a long time in the dark before Mason finally told them to stop.

"Here's far enough," he told Dooley.

Colleen looked up at her surroundings and saw that they were a little ways from the camp that must have been somewhere over the slope they had just walked down, because she couldn't see their campfire anymore. Dooley walked over and tied Colleen's hands together. Then he did the same to Danny. The two men stood together for a moment, watching them and talking in low voices. After a while they both nodded, seeming to have come to an agreement. Colleen looked at Danny and when he looked back at her, she tried to look hopeful for his sake. He looked awfully tired and afraid, and Colleen was almost convinced that this was why Mason had thought he was the boss.

Finally, the two men walked back to them. Dooley grabbed Colleen by the shoulders, and, giving her a little shake, pulled her a few feet away from Danny. Then Mason picked up his gun and aimed it at Danny's chest.

"Since you finally gave yourself up and told me who the boss is," he said, "I might just spare the lives of your men. Yours, on the other hand, is an interference with my plans. You see, I can't take all these cattle to market with you hanging around trying to get the Law involved. So, as much as it pains me, I'm gonna' have to get rid of that interference." His finger was just settling on the trigger when Colleen couldn't prevent herself from doing something other than standing where she was and watching Danny get shot.

"Stop!" she yelled, "Wait! Please, wait."

Mason moved his finger away from the trigger and looked at her. "And why should I wait? The outcome will still be the same."

"Because . . ." Colleen stopped. She still had one trick up her sleeve, but she had never intended to use it. "Because," Danny was shaking his head, shooting her a worried look, "I own the herd," she said in a shaky voice, "They're mine."

"You?" Dooley laughed.

"I don't see someone as young as yourself being able to buy all these cows," Mason said doubtfully.

Colleen decided to go ahead and tell the man the whole truth. There was no reason not to now.

"It's my pa's herd," she explained, "I'm taking them to market for him."

"Really?" Mason said resting his hands on his hips.

Colleen nodded.

"You know, kid, somehow I just don't believe you," he said, then he turned to Danny. "I've got to hand it to you. You're men are the most loyal I've ever seen. Wouldn't you say so, Dooley?"

Dooley murmured his agreement, but his attention was on a short strand of blonde hair peeking out from underneath Colleen's hat. Mason turned back to Danny and Colleen finally gave up. Reaching up with both hands, since her wrists were still tied together, she grabbed the brim of her pa's hat and pulled it off, shaking her head, revealing her dirty blonde hair. Danny stiffened and the two men stared.

"A woman?" Dooley said, somewhere in a state of shock.

"Or a cowboy with long hair," Mason said stepping in closer to Colleen to get a better look at her face. She could feel his eyes scrutinizing every part of her soft but dirty face. Finally, he took a step back then grabbed her face in between two of his thick fingers, pinching her cheeks, and turned to Dooley. "I don't know, what do you think, Dooley? Does she look too ladylike to be out here riding with the menfolk? She's dirty enough." Mason let go of Colleen's face and rubbed his hand on his equally dirty pants.

There was a long silence where Dooley stared at Colleen before he suddenly started to laugh. "I *do* know you!" he said through his laughter. Some of his teeth, Colleen noticed, were yellow or missing.

"She is a lady, Mason. She was the pretty, little girl I saw at the fair back in Morristown. You must love yer pa an awful lot to bring thet perty face out here on this dusty trail. And you're an awful long way from home."

Dooley turned and looked at Danny and his mouth fell open in surprise. "Well call me a jack rabbit."

"Alright, you're a jack rabbit," Mason muttered through a smirk at Colleen.

"*You*," Dooley said pointing an accusing finger at Danny, "were the boy who got in my way at that same fair . . ."

Mason watched quietly as Dooley walked over and stood in front of Danny, aiming the barrel of his gun at Danny's chest. Colleen hadn't thought about him recognizing Danny. Dooley, holding his gun aimed at

Danny, looked over at Colleen as if to see if she would do anything. But before she could say or do anything, Dooley started to laugh his hoarse laugh again. He looked from Colleen back to Danny, and then back to Colleen again. "Oh no," he said mockingly. "You two ain't . . ." He looked at Danny's clenched jaw and breathed out an, "Ahh." He looked as if he had just realized something.

Colleen sucked in a sharp breath and, realizing how defenseless they really were, decided that she would try to run at Mason and get his gun, when no more had her feet started to move toward him than there was a scuffle towards her right and then Branson, Gus, and Fletcher came bursting over the slope, shouting as they tackled Dooley and Mason to the ground. In all the commotion, Colleen heard a gunshot and saw a pile of men, fighting in the dusty moonlight. She quickly found her hat in the dark and, brushing it off, pulled it back on to cover her hair. As the men scrambled around and used the rustlers' ropes to tie them up, Colleen watched, unsure of what to do. The next thing she knew, Mason and Dooley were tied up in rope, and the hands were untangling themselves from the mess of limbs and pulling themselves to their feet and brushing off the dirt.

Colleen checked her hat to make sure it was in its proper place, then she walked over to the two rustlers and stood in front of them. "Where are the other three?" she asked Fletcher over her shoulder.

"Same as these two, Boss," Fletcher answered. "Four to three was pretty easy for us to handle. It was Branson's doing. He had a knife in his vest pocket. He cut the ropes and we tackled 'em, just like we did these two."

"All my days spent out on the range and not once did I ever think to put a knife in my front vest pocket," Gus said shaking his head, "Smart kid."

Colleen glanced over at Branson and he flashed her a wide grin. With a nod to him, she asked, "And Cooks?"

"He's watching them for us," Gus said, then he started laughing. "I doubt they'll try to cross him with that Winchester of his."

"I didn't even know he had a gun," Colleen said as she turned back to Mason and Dooley.

"Every man has a gun in these parts, Boss," Fletcher said.

Colleen remembered her ma telling her before she left that the men she hired would be suspicious of her if she didn't carry one with her. She looked at Mason. "You were right, Mason," she said, "I do have the most loyal men working for me." She turned and walked away from them.

Danny looked at Mason and Dooley. "I never said I was the boss. You came up with that idea on your own."

Colleen looked at Fletcher and Gus and asked them to take the two men back to the camp. "We'll take them with us to Willow Springs," she said, "See what their sheriff has to say about their cattle thieving."

The two hands nodded. Colleen looked at Branson and offered her hand, which he shook after a moment's hesitation.

"Thank you, Branson," she told him.

"Just doing my job and sticking up for the team, Boss," he said.

"I appreciate it," she said, "I know my pa would've been awfully proud of you if he'd been here."

Branson stopped and looked down for a moment, playing with his hat before he looked at her again. "Well, I'm glad to hear that," he said slowly. "Working for your pa was always a privilege. He reminds me a lot of my own pa back east."

Colleen put her hand on his shoulder, hoping it wasn't too womanly of a gesture. "I'm sure your pa would be proud of you too, Branson."

Branson smiled at her and nodded before walking to join the others. Colleen looked over at Danny who was waiting patiently for her, left hand resting on his right shoulder; right hand hanging limply at his side. One look at him told her that something was wrong. Then she saw the little bit of red showing between the fingers of his left hand. She remembered the gunshot and hurried over to him.

"Your arm!" she cried.

"I don't think it's too bad," Danny said waving her away.

"Move your hand and let me see it," Colleen said.

Wincing, Danny carefully removed his hand and Colleen examined the wound. The bullet had just grazed his shoulder, leaving a gash that should heal quickly if they could mend it properly. Colleen took off her bandana and gently tied it on around his arm. She wasn't sure how clean her bandana was, but it was better than nothing.

"Come on," she told him, "Let's see if Cooks has anything to put on your shoulder." She turned and started walking back in the direction she decided their camp was.

"Colleen," Danny said reaching out and stopping her by taking her hand. When she looked at him he hesitated a moment before he said, "Thank you. You didn't have to do that. You didn't have to tell them."

"Yes, I did. I wanted to. After Charles . . ." Colleen looked down and kicked a rock with the toe of her boot, "It just seemed like the right thing to do, that's all."

Danny nodded.

"Let's just hope that Mason and Dooley don't tell the hands all they found out," Colleen said.

After a moment, Danny looked to his left, then back at Colleen. "Oh, and um . . . camp is that way," he said pointing south. A moment ago, Colleen had started to go west. Realizing her mistake, she smiled sheepishly and Danny grinned.

"I thought that looked different," she said suppressing a giggle. The long day was finally starting to get to her. Colleen turned towards camp a second time, but then stopped, realizing that Danny was still holding her hand. She looked down at their hands and noticed how small her newly calloused hand was compared to his strong one. She felt her heart suddenly start beating faster than it had been and looked up from their hands to Danny's face. Their eyes met and he quickly let go.

THIRTEEN

Cooks did have something for Danny's shoulder. But when he tended to the wound, Colleen left the covered wagon, not being able to stand the tears of pain in Danny's eyes. She was so glad when Danny was finally better and healed enough to be able to ride using his right hand to guide his horse again. And Danny seemed to be happy to be himself again too. The hands teased Danny and Colleen about who they should be calling the boss since the rustlers — who were tied up in the back of Cooks' wagon and would remain so until they reached the Sheriff's office in Willow Springs — had thought Danny was the owner of the cattle. They especially liked to joke about it to each other in front of the rustlers.

"The best part of this," Fletcher said, one day when they were about a day out from Willow Springs, and stopping at a creek to get some fresh water and to let the cattle drink, "Is that they have to ride the rest of the way with us," he gestured to the rustlers, "but they won't be getting paid one cent for it." Branson laughed, looking over at the rustlers where their horses were tied to the back of Cooks' wagon.

"Yeah, and who were we supposed to be calling the boss, again?" Cooks asked, laughing.

Colleen shook her head as she splashed her face with cool creek water, no longer concerned with having to smear dirt on her face to hide her true identity — the rain had washed it all off long ago, anyway. The hands had done it again. Turned a regular conversation into that made the miserable rustlers look foolish. She knew there was nothing respectable about the men, but she also had the feeling that she should encourage her own men not to make fun of them in their misery. It wasn't the right kind of example to be setting.

Only then, did she hear Gus say, in answer to Cooks' question about who they should call the boss, "Well, it'll either be Danny or Colleen—"

There was a collective silence in their group as what he said registered with the other men. Colleen's head snapped around as she looked at Gus, then turned to Danny, the only other person who had known besides the rustlers. But since the rustlers were gagged . . . Danny too, was looking at Gus, then slowly, he set down the harness he was working with and looked at Colleen.

"You told Gus?" she said in a voice barely above a whisper.

She had mixed feelings on the matter. One was of relief, one was concern, and another frustration. Danny didn't answer, he just looked over at the hands, looking slightly uncomfortable. The hands just stared at their boots looking guilty while Cooks started stammering, trying to say something reassuring to her. She looked around at them all standing there with their hats in their hands, some staring at their boots, others looking at her like guilty children.

"You *all* knew?" she asked in disbelief.

"We was just tryin' to help you, miss," Branson said quietly.

Colleen couldn't help flinching when he said *miss*. She was so used to hearing the names Callen or Boss or Mr. Northam, when being referred to by the hands, that *miss* sounded almost foreign. Colleen turned and walked around to the other side of the covered wagon to gather her thoughts. With a look at the hands, Danny walked past the miserable-looking rustlers and followed her. He had no more than rounded the side of the wagon when Colleen turned around and seeing who it was, pulled him into a hug. When she let go, Danny stepped back to get a good look at her face. He had assumed she would be angry at him for telling the men.

Colleen took a deep breath, then said, "So you told them?"

"Yes, but it was before you asked me not to," Danny answered.

Colleen suddenly remembered the smile Danny had given her when he had told her not to worry about him telling the men about her. Of course, she hadn't needed to worry about it. Because he had already told them.

"Well, wait, how long have they known, then?" she asked.

"Ever since the night I figured it out, for myself," Danny answered. At the look on Colleen's face, he explained, "I figured it was only fair that they know who they were working for. I told them if they wanted to quit then I'd pay them extra for helping drive the herd to market, and for not giving you a hard time or telling you they knew about it. I figured me being a man and all, would convince them that they would still get their fair share of the money."

"And they agreed to that?" she asked.

"In the beginning, several of them wanted the extra money," Danny said thoughtfully, "But since Charles asked you to say that prayer, something's definitely changed because they've all said that they don't want the extra money anymore. Must be those Sunday morning meetings of yours."

Colleen smiled as she thought of the last three Sundays, and how the hands had been so eager to hear her quote another scripture or two. And ever since Charles' death, they had shared saying the prayer before breakfast every morning. Over the weeks, everyone had taken turns — some of them learning how to pray for the first time. And several times, they had asked her to repeat Psalm 23. The chapter from the Bible that she had quoted at Charles' grave for his funeral.

"The good Lord knows what He's doing," Colleen said finally. "Just like when He put me out here on this trail. Maybe it wasn't so much for my pa or my family as it was for these men."

"Well, He couldn't have picked a better person," Danny said. "Now we best be getting those cows back on the trail. But before we do, you should probably tell the fellas that you're not mad at them . . . or me."

Colleen smiled, then suddenly she remembered something that she had been wanting to ask him for some time now. "Danny, when did you figure out that it was me? That I wasn't Mr. Northam's son," she asked.

"I suspected when I first heard you talk about what had happened to your pa, when you hired me for the job," Danny said, "And when I didn't see you with your family the morning we left, I figured there were only two options. That either you were Colleen, or you were married. So when I asked you that night and you reacted the way you did, I put it together. And I decided that your best way of surviving was if I helped you. That's another reason I told the men. That way they wouldn't find out on their own and quit, leaving you out here by yourself with all these cows."

"You're only helping me so I can survive?" Colleen asked quietly.

"No," Danny said then stopped himself as he looked at her more carefully.

"Then why are you helping me?" Colleen asked. She felt a chill run through her, but it wasn't from being cold. If anything, it was terribly hot out under the fierce sun.

After a minute, Danny answered, "I guess it's my turn to let you figure that out."

Colleen looked at him uncertainly. "Well, I guess I'll have to start working on it, then," she said.

With a grin, Danny stepped closer to the wagon, allowing her to pass by him so she could go talk to the other hands.

FOURTEEN

The morning they would be reaching Willow Springs, Colleen woke with a start inside her tent, having slept far past the time that she was usually up at. She scolded herself for not waking on time, then blamed it on the fact that she hadn't slept much the night that the rustlers had tried to steal the cattle, and she was still trying to catch up on her sleep. Of course, this wasn't a good enough reason, so she blamed it on the fact that she had been sleeping on the ground for almost a month. Oh how she couldn't wait to get home and just do her chores and act feminine, and wear pretty skirts and hair ribbons again. She even didn't mind the thought of callers, as long as she could be sleeping in her own bed again, with no cattle to worry about. Colleen tucked her hair up underneath her hat again, because even though the hands might know who she was, no one else could. It was shameful for a woman to wear a man's clothing, even if it was to save her family's ranch. She pulled on her gun belt and tied down her gun. She now considered her gun as a more valuable piece of her attire since the rustlers had shown up, just like Danny had told her she would. Unfortunately, the night the rustlers had come to take the cattle, she had already taken her gun and belt off. But now she kept it close. Danny seemed to know quite a bit about driving cattle and the trail, Colleen noticed. It's no wonder Mason had thought he was the man in charge. Colleen wondered how long he had been working as a cowpoke.

She hurriedly rolled up her blanket, put on her vest and buttoned it, then packed up her tent. When she had found Cooks, she saw that he was letting the rustlers eat their breakfast before setting out dishes for everyone else. Colleen had the thought that it was kind of like a farm feeding the livestock before eating his own breakfast. Colleen couldn't help but smile a little at the idea of these rustlers being like livestock. Cooks informed her that Branson had gone out to check the cattle. Colleen nodded and helped Cooks with the breakfast preparations until all the hands were standing around waiting for Branson to come back from checking the cattle. When he didn't show, and twenty minutes had passed, Colleen began to feel uneasy about his absence. Finally, Danny looked at them all and stood up.

"I'll go see if I can find him," he volunteered.

Colleen watched as he rode off in the direction of the herd; in the distance she could see the cattle. They seemed a little restless. Suddenly, she spotted a cloud of dust behind the herd, and about the time she saw it, she felt the ground tremor under her feet. The men all looked up, their faces going pale. Colleen wasn't sure what it was that they recognized about the sound and the cloud of dust, but she did know it wasn't anything good. The men were suddenly on their horses riding towards the herd at a full gallop. Colleen found and saddled Daisy faster than she ever had before and was about to follow the men when Cooks gently put a hand on her arm.

"Be careful, ma'am," he said, "looks like there could be a stampede."

At the word 'stampede', a new fear shot through Colleen and she turned Daisy toward the sound, urging her into a gallop. Eyes wide, hands clenched to fists around the reins, Colleen urged Daisy faster, praying and thinking about how in the last few days they had traveled into an area of rocks, hills, and dangerous cliffs that dropped off to nowhere. If those cows started toward one of those cliffs . . .

"Oh, God," Colleen prayed, "Me and the men need strength and wisdom, now more than ever. Lord, help us to stop those cows."

When she reached the herd, that was indeed in a full stampede now, she saw that the hands were riding alongside the cattle, trying to turn them westward. Not too far north, she saw that there was a cliff, and the cattle were headed straight for it!

Colleen rode down to the edge of the herd, trying to keep up with the cattle, and yet get to where Danny was riding up ahead of her. Colleen leaned down close to Daisy's neck, sweat and dust, mixing in a terrible taste in her mouth. She hadn't known that cows could run so fast. When she got close to Danny, she yelled his name. Danny looked back at her and slowed his horse just enough to let her catch up.

"What do we do?" she yelled to him, still keeping pace with the cattle.

"We've gotta try to turn them, before they reach the cliff!" he yelled back.

"How?" she shouted.

"If we can get to the cliff before they do and make some noise, it might be enough to scare them so that they turn away from the sound," Danny said, "But if we don't hurry, we could be too late and lose the whole herd!"

Colleen pulled back on Daisy's reins, slowing her to a speed that she could turn her around at.

"Colleen!" Danny shouted at her.

"I can't lose this herd," she yelled back at him, but she doubted he heard her now over the hooves of the cattle and horses.

Colleen had an idea about what kind of scary noise would turn the cattle, but she had to get there in time for it to work. She pushed Daisy hard, back the way they had come from, praying that she would make it to the cliff before the cattle did, and praying that Daisy would not get hurt from this ride. She just knew that she couldn't lose the herd on the very last day before they made it to market.

Finally, she reached the back of the herd and turned Daisy alongside the stampeding cattle. It was now a race to the edge of the cliff. Something Colleen kept thinking about, was Danny asking her if she knew hot to shoot, and it's from there that she had gotten her idea for noise. Colleen neared the front of the cattle, passing Branson — thanking God that he was okay since he had probably been in the herd when they had first started their stampede — and Gus, and not long after she passed up the front of the herd, she could see the place where the ground ended in a drop off. Slowing Daisy, she rode as close as she dared to the edge of the cliff, then stopped her horse and pulling her gun out of its holster, aimed it at the sky, realizing that if the cattle didn't stop, or turn, they would run her and Daisy right off the cliff with them. Colleen looked back at the frightened faces of the cows, and without hesitation, squeezed the trigger. She blinked at the sound of the gunshot and her arm jerked back. She didn't dare look at the cows now as she fired a second shot into the air.

The herd kept running, she could tell that by the rumbling sound that continued after she fired her gun. But when she was able to make herself look at the cattle, she saw that they were not stampeding straight towards her anymore. They had apparently heard the sound of the gunshots and had turned at the last minute. Branson and Gus rode with the herd, cracking their whips to keep them turning. Gus nodded at Colleen as they flashed by her, apparently pleased with what she had done. Deep down, Colleen realized the new respect she had for her fellow cowboys. They did this all the time out on the trails. She realized, too, that there was a reason God had made her a woman, because she wouldn't be able to take another frightening experience like that one, or like the one with the rustlers, for a long time.

When she had caught her breath, Colleen joined the others again. It took a long time to wear the cattle down so that they stopped stampeding, and when they did finally come to a stop, Colleen and the hands were worn out, sweaty, and hungry. Colleen volunteered to watch the cattle while the others ate breakfast, even though the cattle were so tired themselves they weren't likely to be going much of anywhere. The hands didn't want to go eat breakfast without her, but she finally told them that it would be awhile before she could make herself eat anything. Her adrenaline and emotions were still running so high from chasing the herd and trying to keep them from running off the cliff that she felt sick. At the moment, the thought of food was not appetizing. So the hands all agreed to let her stay out and watch the herd while they ate a quick breakfast at the newly repositioned covered wagon. That was the only good part about the stampede, if such a thing was possible. They had fortunately been able to turn the cattle in the direction of the market, and Cooks had just followed at a distance with the wagon full of food supplies. Colleen now guessed them to be about four hours out from Willow Springs. They would soon be able to sell the cows and make their preparations for the return journey home. At the thought of home, Colleen's heart leapt in anticipation, but then she pushed the thought away so that she would be able to focus on what was before her instead. After Cooks was able to talk Colleen into consuming a decent breakfast, they set out for market for the last time on their long journey, and four hours later, they rode into Willow Springs. Colleen silently prayed and thanked God for getting them there without any more mishaps.

The first thing they did was sell the cattle. Part of Colleen was glad that the pay was good and it made her happy to not have to worry about them anymore, but the other part of her was almost sad to see them go, because of all the good things that had happened because of that herd. With one last glance at her pa's cows — her cows — she turned and walked away. Her and the hands took the five rustlers to the Willow Springs sheriff office where the Sheriff thanked them and said he'd been looking for Mason and Dooley for a while. The others, Colleen learned, were called Jebediah, Craig, and Anderson. But as the Sheriff locked them up, one at a time, Dooley made it a point to tell them — with Mason telling him to hush — all about their other hand who had been trying to get away from him in the rain, when his horse slipped and fell, and he hit his head on a rock.

"But unfortunately, in all the rain, we still weren't able to grab the herd," Dooley said with a smirk. "Guess it wasn't our year . . . Coward."

"Dooley, would you shut up," Mason said as the Sheriff led him inside.

Colleen stared at Dooley blankly as the words he'd said settled in. He meant Charles who hadn't just had an accident. He had been running, trying to get away from the rustlers, possibly even trying to warn the rest of them that they were there, and had slipped in the rain, hitting his head on that rock. Because of these men. Colleen started shaking, and the news affected the other hands as well. Fletcher's brow creased as he stared at the man. Cooks muttered something under his breath. Branson shook his head and Danny's face went pale.

Suddenly, Colleen was aware of only Gus as he moved toward Dooley. He seemed much taller now than he had before, and he leveled his gaze at the harsh face of the even harsher man before him.

"'But now you boast in your arrogance,'" he quoted in his low, gravelly voice, a verse Colleen recognized from the book of James in the Bible, "You caused a young man to lose his life because of your greed. Too selfish to think of him or his family. I used to be just like you, except I made sure that no man lost his life for my cause. And then one day, I came across a Man who did lose His life for my cause. A Man I'd never met before, who didn't deserve to die, but did because He loved me."

Gus looked at him steadily as Dooley smirked. "Are you talkin' 'bout your God?" he asked sarcastically.

Gus laid a gentle hand on the man's shoulder. "I'll pray that you find Him too." With that, he let his hand drop to his side and the Sheriff nodded to them and took Dooley inside his office and locked him up too. Everyone was silent and Colleen stared at Gus's back, realizing that he had just shared his testimony with not only all of them, but with a thief and a murderer, and the Sheriff heard it too. Slowly, they all turned away and started walking back into town, saddened by the news of what had really happened to Charles, except that Colleen and Gus stayed where they were. Gus turned around and looked at her.

"I wanted so bad to punch him in the nose," he said.

"You did the right thing, Gus," Colleen assured him. "However, had you hit him, I just hope It would have been hard enough to knock some sense into him."

Gus smiled.

"Oh, it would've been," he said.

FIFTEEN

The rest of that day was spent preparing for the journey home. Colleen and Cooks went shopping at the Willow Springs General Store for supplies. Cooks stocked up on food items since his supply had been eaten down due to feeding five extra people, and Colleen bought some patch equipment for her saddlebags since one had recently developed a small hole in the corner. Before they left the store, Colleen walked to where the bolts of fabric were, and ran a soft hand over a dark blue one. There was a pale yellow one to the right of the blue one, and to the left there was a pink one. There were many other surrounding those three and Colleen was just thinking of what her ma could do with all the pretty bolts of fabric — especially the pale green one with the lilac flowers on it; it would make such a beautiful bonnet — when the store owner's wife, Mrs. Brady, walked up to her and said, "Are you considerin' purchasing somethin' for yer missus back home?"

If only she knew, Colleen thought as a smile crossed her face. But she said, "No, ma'am. I'm not married. I was just thinking 'bout my ma."

The lady looked more into Colleen's face and squinted, making Colleen slightly nervous as she did so. But the lady just shrugged and said, "I guess you are a little young to be married, but you know sometimes folks do get married at your age."

At the look on Colleen's face, the woman laughed lightly. "Oh my," she said, "Here I am talking like a woman to a cowboy. I'm sorry, you probably don't enjoy chatter. Just let me know if you'd like to purchase anything." With one last smile, the lady walked away, leaving Colleen shaking her head and thinking once more, *If only she knew*. She also realized how long it had been since she had even spoken to a woman. *It would have been nice to talk longer*, she thought. With one last glance at the bolts of fabric, Colleen turned toward the door and started out onto the porch in front of the store. The other hands and Cooks stood outside talking as they waited for her. Cooks had apparently finished his shopping. Danny stood leaning against the doorway and watched her as she walked out.

"You have everything you want?" he asked her. And although Colleen noticed that he said *want* and not *need*, she just nodded, her mind still on those bolts of fabric.

At Danny's suggestion, they spent the night camping outside Willow Springs. That night, Colleen paid them all their share of the money that they had made from the herd and afterwards, Danny went back into town, and Fletcher quietly approached her and told her that in the morning he was hoping to stay in Willow Springs if that was alright with her. Colleen told him that it was, but they would miss him on the way home. The cattle had sold well and everyone's pay was good, but there was one bundle of cash that Colleen packed away for when she got home. This money had been meant for Charles, but Colleen now set it aside for his family, if she could find them when she got home.

That evening was a quiet one, as they all eventually heard from Fletcher that he would not be returning home with them. But Colleen tried to keep everyone cheerful for Fletcher's sake. He clearly wanted to stay and she didn't want to stop him just because they would all miss him on the way back to Morristown. And she certainly didn't want his last night with them to be spent in sad silence. So she kept the hands talking through dinner — which was a little fancier than the normal grub they had out on the trail — then Colleen ran out of things to say. She had told them stories of her family, she knew a few jokes that her pa had told her once upon a time, but mostly she tried to get each one of them to talk about themselves and their families, if they had one. She learned that Gus rode as a cattle hand because he didn't have a family, his wife had died almost twenty years ago, and they hadn't had children yet, so he had taken to the trails and had stayed there for as long as Colleen had been alive. Fletcher didn't say much more than why he wanted to stay in Willow Springs, which was to start up his own ranch out West. Branson had a wife and two young children back in Morristown. He announced that although he liked working with cattle, he prefered being a sodbuster so he could be closer to his family. Not as many cattle drives, unless they needed the money and he chose to go. Cooks said he never had much of a family to begin with. He had lived back east and his parents had died when he was young; he never married, and he said he liked the prairie, so after a few years out west, he chose never to return east. "I'm a travelin' man," he said proudly, "and I'm jest fine with that."

The men also asked Colleen about her family, and now that she had nothing to hide from them, she told them about her ma and pa and her four younger siblings. She also told them about why she had come out west with the cattle, and told them about her pa's accident, and the telegram she'd received in Ellington about his condition. The hands all assured her that he would be almost healed by the time she got back home, and Colleen smiled at their encouraging words, hoping that maybe they would be true. It was late when Danny came back from town and ate the leftovers from the meal that Cooks had made, since he'd missed supper. Colleen wanted to ask him where he'd been, but she knew that no matter their friendship at the moment, it was none of her business, so she said nothing and turned in for the night.

The next morning, she woke up to Danny standing outside her tent, telling her to wake up. At first she panicked because she thought she had overslept again, but Danny said that he just wanted to show her something. So she quickly got up and packed her things, then mounted her horse and followed Danny. Most of the hands weren't up yet when they left, and Cooks smiled at Colleen as he told her that breakfast would be ready when they got back. Colleen was surprised when Danny took her back into town. She was even more surprised when they stopped at the General Store and Danny knocked on the door since they weren't open yet, telling Colleen to wait outside for a minute. The door opened and the store owner beckoned him in and a few minutes later, Danny waved Colleen in. Once she walked inside, Danny closed the door behind them and she heard the store owner mutter something as he walked away, like, "The missus was up half the night tryin' to finish that." Then he told Danny to let him know when he was done so he could let them back out of the store. Colleen turned to Danny in confusion about what they were doing in the General Store so early that the store wasn't even open yet. She was about to ask when she noticed that Danny was holding a rather large parcel in his hands. Slowly Danny turned and gave the package to Colleen.

"It's a gift for you. There's a room back there for you to open it in, I think," he told her.

Even more confused, Colleen turned toward the back of the store and sure enough, there was a small room with a door that Colleen quietly closed. She turned to the package and slowly, carefully, began to open it, wondering as she did so, what could possibly be inside. But when she saw what was in it, she couldn't prevent the tears from welling up in her eyes. Inside the package was a navy blue skirt, a pink blouse, and a bonnet made of the green and purple lilacs fabric she had seen in the store, the day before. There were also a few undergarments in the bottom of the package to go along with the skirt and top. Colleen sat down on the small chair that graced the room with its presence and pulled all three items onto her lap. This gift from Danny was something she had never even thought about, that she would be able to return home dressed as the woman she was.

Brushing away her tears, Colleen pulled off her hat and braided her hair. It had grown some since when she'd cut it and fell down below her shoulder blades. She twisted the blonde locks into a tight bun, hoping it would hold its place. It had been a while since she had fixed her hair in such a ladylike style. She quickly changed out of her cowboy clothes and dressed in the new, feminine ones. *This must've been what that kind lady stayed up so late working on*, Colleen thought fondly as she remembered the woman. "Oh, it must have cost Danny a fortune," she said to herself as she tied on the bonnet and folded up her other things. When she found herself ready, she opened the door of the small room and went to find Danny. He stood by the counter at the front of the store and didn't hear her walk up, so she said in her normal voice, "What do you think?"

He quickly turned around and once he saw her, he just looked at her. Colleen suddenly felt as if she were back at the fair in Morristown, looking at the young man who had never said anything to her; the stranger, who was no longer a stranger to her, but instead, someone she depended on and cared about. Only this time she didn't feel the need to look away from his blue eyes. To cover up the sound of her heart beating too quickly, she asked, "Well?"

Suddenly, Danny smiled. "I always knew that a pretty face like yours couldn't belong to some rancher."

Colleen laughed before she remembered that she was supposed to be quiet since the store wasn't yet open and Mrs. Brady was probably still sleeping since she'd stayed up so late making all these fine clothes.

"I should thank Mrs. Brady for... When did you ask her to make these?" She asked Danny.

"I came in last night after you paid us, and picked out the colors I saw you looking at yesterday. Then I asked Mr. Brady's wife to sew you a bonnet and an outfit. From the looks of it she's pretty good at that sort of thing. I was pretty nervous asking someone I wasn't sure knew how to sew to make them for you, but it looks like the only choice I had was the best one I could've made anyway," he said.

"I'll pay you for it when I get back home," she said.

"No need. Like I said, it's a gift," Danny said.

"You sure?"

"Quite."

"Thank you," Colleen said and she meant it with all her heart.

Danny smiled at her. "You're welcome."

After finding Mr. Brady and thanking him, Danny offered Colleen his arm and she took it graciously, thankful to finally be able to act like a lady.

After breakfast, and saying farewell to Fletcher, Colleen and the hands mounted up for the ride home that would hopefully take much less time than their journey to Willow Springs, since they no longer had any cows to drive, and hopefully there wouldn't be any rain storms this time. The whole journey home, Colleen thought of her family and wondered how her pa was doing by now. They didn't take the time to stop in Ellington so she wasn't able to send a telegram. The closer she got to her home, the more excited she felt every morning and every night, and then finally, one day as they rode, Colleen began to recognize her surroundings again. She was almost home. She had to hold herself back from urging Daisy into a gallop. But it still didn't take them very long before Colleen saw her ma and pa's house in the distance. And then, no longer able to hold herself or Daisy back, since Daisy seemed to be just as excited to get back to her personal stall in the barn, she let Daisy gallop the whole way down the hill and into the yard.

At the sound of horses in the yard, the house door burst open and Colleen was in her ma's arms before she even realized she had gotten out of her saddle and landed on the ground. Then, there was her pa, walking slowly towards her, the brightest smile she'd ever seen him give lighting up his whole face as he asked, "Where's my sweet girl?" Colleen was embracing him when the hands rode into the yard, followed by Cooks in the covered wagon. And that's when her ma seemed to notice that something was off.

"Colleen, where are . . ." her ma started, then lowered her voice. "Where are your other clothes?"

Colleen glanced back at the hands and smiled.

"They figured out who I really am, Mama," she said meeting Danny's tired, but happy smile before looking back at her ma. "But they helped me, even after they found out."

Colleen's ma looked so relieved, Colleen was worried she might faint.

"I prayed that either they would never suspect you, or that if they did find out, you would be safe and that God would help you the whole time," her ma told her taking her face in her hands.

"He did, Mama," Colleen said. "He did."

"Then one night when I was praying with your pa, he remembered a verse and we both started reading it every time we thought about you," her ma said, "It was Romans eight, verse twenty-eight."

"'And we know that all things work together for good to them that love God, to them who are called according to His purpose," Colleen quoted. That scripture had been one that she had memorized as a small child.

Her ma smiled. "You remember it," she said.

"Of course I do. But I was thinking more along the lines of Psalm twenty-three," Colleen said, getting a whoop from the hands. She smiled at them and then turned to her pa. "Are you feeling better?" she asked him as the hands dismounted.

"I feel about as good as new thanks to the doc, and now that you're here," he said, then his face grew serious. "How can I ever thank you enough, my sweet daughter? You saved our whole family, *and* our ranch."

"You don't have to thank me, Pa," Colleen answered, "I wasn't the one who made everything work out. That was all God's doing, and everything else was thanks to these hands here, because I had no clue what I was doing out there. But they showed me and God paved the way."

"You're right," her pa said with a smile, "We have a lot to be praising Him for."

"Well, instead of standing around with empty stomachs," Colleen's ma said, "I'll go and cook us up some fried chicken, and you can invite all the hands in, if you like Jethro."

"I think Colleen should," her pa said proudly, "they're her cowpokes, not mine."

Colleen giggled. "But your money hired them to work for me."

"Alright, alright," her pa laughed, "then I'll do the invitin' and you go on in the house with your mama. I know you're tired, and besides, the boys are dying to see you."

"Okay," Colleen said still smiling.

How good it felt to be home. She could barely stand to hold the joy of it all. She heard her pa invite the hands for supper as she started for the house. Then she remembered Daisy and walked back to her horse as the men graciously accepted the invitation to supper.

"It'd be right nice to have someone cook for me since I usually do all the cooking," Cooks said and everyone laughed.

Branson was the only one who declined to eat supper with them. He said he had just a short ride home and wanted to see his wife and children before it got too dark and he couldn't travel. So with a nod to the other cowboys, a shake of her pa's hand, and a wink at Colleen, he went off towards home and Colleen prayed that he would get there quickly and safely.

When Danny offered to put Daisy in the barn for her, Colleen caught her pa looking between the two of them curiously. Colleen remembered what Danny had once told her about him knowing and working for her pa when he was younger, and Colleen wondered if perhaps he recognized Danny, but she didn't give it much thought after that. Instead, she let Danny bed her horse down for the night and she went in the house to give hugs and kisses and head pats to Joey, Aaron, Riley, and Abigail Rose.

That night, the Northam house was full of people, joy, and laughter as they all took turns telling some of the stories of the things that had happened out on the trail. When Charles was mentioned, everyone grew quiet and solemn. Colleen learned from her ma that word had been sent to his family, through the Doc, as she had asked. On the way home, Colleen and the hands had stopped by the place where they had buried him and Colleen picked some wildflowers to put by the marker Gus had made for the young man. Just thinking about it made her want to weep. He had been so young, had just come to know the Lord, and the rustlers — they now knew — had been the ones to make him lose that. *Well*, Colleen thought, *no, he didn't lose* all *of it*. He was with the Lord now, and no one could ever take that away from him. Colleen looked at Danny for a moment, wondering if he was remembering that stop at Charles' grave too. She wondered too, how the rustlers were doing in Willow Springs. Perhaps they weren't even in Willow Springs anymore, that might have been moved to a bigger town by now, but who knew. She just hoped that they realized that what they had done was wrong and changed for the better before it was too late.

Finally, Colleen's ma announced that it was time for bed and so, bidding their family goodnight, the hands went outside to sleep in the attic of the barn while her ma put the boys and Abigail Rose — who had long since fallen asleep on her mother's lap, overcome with excitement and exhaustion — to bed. Colleen's pa looked over at her, a thoughtful expression on his face. They had been talking about how life had been for her as one of the cowboys and she had just run out of things to say before more came spilling to the front of her mind, but her pa interrupted her with his next sentence.

"That Danny LaHaye seems to be a nice young man," he said.

"He is, Pa," Colleen agreed, "Out of all of them he was the one who helped me the most because he figured out who I was the soonest. And . . ." she hesitated, thinking back, "he was the cowboy who won the race at the fair a few months ago. The one who protected me from that man. The rustler."

"Really?" her pa said in surprise, "Well, who would've ever thought?" After a minute, he added, "What do you think of him?"

Colleen smiled, "Lots of things . . . At first. Now, it's more like just one thing."

"And what is that one thing?" her pa asked with a gentle smile.

"Well . . . It's hard to explain," Colleen answered slowly, "I like him now. I just never can seem to find a way to describe it. Even to myself."

"Hmm," her pa said, a frown creased his forehead as he thought, then he said, "You know, I think he likes you too."

Colleen looked at him for a long moment seeing the understanding in his eyes before asking, "How do you know?"

"I can tell by the way he looks at you. The respect he has for you," he answered.

Not knowing what to say, Colleen just smiled again and fell silent as her ma joined them again, asking all about their journey, but what her pa said about Danny liking her too lingered in her mind for some time afterward. That night, she lay down in her bed, thankful for how soft it felt to her back, her neck, and all her other aching limbs. The first week out on the trail had been the worst, she remembered. And the first day especially; all she had wanted to do was just go to bed and fall asleep in the food Cooks had prepared. She had never even thought about the physical part of being out on the trail and doing the job of a cowboy because she had watched the herd at home so many times, but nothing could have prepared her for the harshness of the trail. The second day, it had been all she could do not to fall asleep in her saddle. But slowly she had toughened up and now she was back home, safe and sound; the adventure over. And she was pretty sure the hands were glad to get off the hard ground too. Colleen smiled into her pillow. She was going to miss them all so much.

SIXTEEN

Colleen bid her hands goodbye the very next morning after breakfast. She wore the skirt and blouse that Danny had bought her, but she didn't wear her bonnet. Instead she wore her hair down, loose, for the first time since she had left to drive the cattle to market. She bid both Gus and Cooks goodbye and thanked them, and they rode off together, Gus on horseback and Cooks in the covered wagon. She hoped she would see them both around Morristown again soon. Cooks had talked about actually settling down in their nice town, and Gus said that the man was so used to traveling that he wouldn't, and they both left the Northam's ranch debating about who would be likely to settle down first and both denying that it would be them. Colleen's family had said their goodbyes and their thanks right after breakfast so that now Colleen was the only one out in the yard to see the men off. She waved to Gus and Cooks one last time, then slowly, she turned to Danny who stood with his horse beside him, ready to leave her life just as quickly and suddenly as he had walked into it. Out of all the goodbyes she had had to say, this one was the worst, and she had dreaded it the most.

"Well, I'll be seeing you around," Danny said.

Colleen wondered if his heart was hurting him like hers was hurting her.

"Yeah," she almost whispered, then louder, "I guess so."

Danny nodded.

Colleen suddenly thought of something she should say, and should have said a long time ago at the fair. "Danny, I want to thank you," she said making herself look at him, "For everything. I know you helped me out on the trail, and bought me these clothes. And I know you won't let me, but I still think I should pay you back for them . . . But it's more than all that," she said glancing down at her skirt and blouse that he had paid Mrs. Brady to make for her.

"It's more than all that," she said again. "I should have thanked you long ago for helping me at the fair too. It may not have seemed like much to you at the time, but it meant — means — a lot to me. So, thank you."

"Colleen," Danny said softly, "You don't have to thank me for that, more than anything I was big on myself for helping you at the fair. I wanted to be the hero and save the day to impress you, as boyish as that sounds. And on the trail, there were several times you helped me too. Actually, I don't think there's anything to be thanking me for. And no, I won't let you pay me for the clothes. But I guess you can still thank me if it makes you feel better."

Colleen smiled. Selfishly, she thought about asking him to stay, but of course, she knew that she couldn't do that. So instead she reached out and hugged him tight. He hugged her back even tighter and when she let go, he reached up gently and touched her cheek. Colleen felt shivers all down her arms as she looked into his eyes. She suddenly wondered if perhaps the feeling she felt whenever she looked at him wasn't something deeper than she'd ever thought it could be. She'd never felt this way about any other person.

Danny took his hand away and gave her a small smile. "I have to leave."

"I'll miss you," Colleen said.

"You won't miss me for long," he said stepping away and climbing up onto his horse.

"You sound so sure," Colleen said.

Danny smiled as he fixed his hat on his head. "I'm planning on coming back by later on in the week."

"You are?" Colleen asked, suddenly filled with hope.

"Yup, I was hoping to talk to your pa about coming to call on his daughter," Danny said and grinned. "That is," he added, "If she'll have me, and if she's not off on some cattle drive."

Colleen laughed delightedly. "I don't think she'll be doing any more of those, and I'm sure she'll be happy to have you," she said.

"Good," Danny said, "then she'll be here when I come calling."

Colleen nodded, holding back tears of joy.

"I'll miss you too," Danny said, then urging his horse forward, he rode off, looking back to wave at her.

Colleen waved to him, knowing now that it was love she felt for him. Although it was just the beginning. Now that she knew he would be coming back to call on her, all she would have to do was wait until their next meeting. As she watched him ride away, she realized that her long journey, that had been so blessed, had finally come to a joyous end.

WESTWARD JOURNEY

THE END.

WESTWARD JOURNEY

Acknowledgements

First and foremost, I want to thank Jesus Christ for all the many blessings I receive daily and for this story idea. It was a joy to write down on paper.

I want to thank my family for being with me every step of the way and for supporting my aspiration as an author. I especially want to thank my mother and father who proof read my stories, give me ideas and offer suggestions.

I also want to thank the long list of people who have inspired me and been so helpful throughout this entire process. My editor and all my critique partners who have talked me through the hard parts of getting my book published. Thank you all!

With that said, I hope you, dear reader, have enjoyed this story as much I did writing it, and will share this story with your family and friends.

Blessings,

Anastasia S. Tarkington

WESTWARD JOURNEY

About the Author

ANASTASIA S. TARKINGTON started writing stories when she was very young. *Westward Journey* is her debut novel. She is an experienced musician, teacher, and takes on the role of photographer in her free time. Anastasia lives in Arkansas with her family and is currently working on her latest story idea.

WESTWARD JOURNEY